FOR LYNDIE, THE TRUTH IS COMPLICATED

"Did Daddy come home?"

"He has business," Lady says. "In Knoxville. He'll be home when he's home."

"What kind of business," I say. "Ma didn't say he had business."

"That's not your concern."

"*Why* is Daddy in Knoxville?" I kick at the floorboards in frustration. "Nobody ever tells me the damn truth."

"Don't you dare use language with me. Stop that kicking right now. Do *you* tell the truth, Lyndie Hawkins? Do you? Or do you tell it only when it suits you?"

I stare out the window.

"Oh mercy," Lady says. "What did I do to be burdened with such a child? My sweet mother must be looking down from heaven and raining tears."

Here it comes again.

"Let's hope Great-Grandma keeps crying through the dry season," I say. "At least the carrots and green beans will stay watered."

OTHER BOOKS YOU MAY ENJOY

THE TRUE HISTORY OF LYNDIE B. HAWKINS

GAIL SHEPHERD

DIAL BOOKS FOR YOUNG READERS

Dial Books for Young Readers
An imprint of Penguin Random House LLC, New York

First published in the United States of America by Kathy Dawson Books
Published by Puffin Books, an imprint of Penguin Random House LLC, 2020

This edition published 2021
Copyright © 2019 by Gail Shepherd

Visit us online at penguinrandomhouse.com

THE LIBRARY OF CONGRESS HAS CATALOGED THE KATHY DAWSON BOOKS EDITION AS FOLLOWS:
Names: Shepherd, Gail, author.
Title: The true history of Lyndie B. Hawkins / Gail Shepherd.
Description: New York, NY : Kathy Dawson Books, [2019] | Summary: When twelve-year-
old Lyndie and her parents must move to her grandparents' home in small-town Tennessee
in 1985, having to keep all family problems private only adds to their problems. | Identifiers:
LCCN 2018009940| ISBN 9780525428459 (hardcover) | ISBN 9780698189218 (ebook)
Subjects: | CYAC: Secrets—Fiction. | Veterans—Fiction. | Grandparents—Fiction. |
Foster children—Fiction. | Family life—Tennessee—Fiction. | Tennessee—History—20th
century—Fiction. | Classification: LCC PZ7.1.S51447 Tru 2019 | DDC [Fic]—dc23
LC record available at https://lccn.loc.gov/2018009940

ISBN 9780147515612

Printed in the United States of America
Designed by Jennifer Kelly
Text set in Life BT Roman

3 5 7 9 10 8 6 4 2

FOR MY MOTHER, JUNE SHEPHERD.

THE READER.

There is such a thing as honorable lying. Take the folks who lied to the authorities to protect enslaved people on the Underground Railroad. I'm sure if there is a St. Peter, he waved those liars right through the Pearly Gates when they finally arrived to heaven.

What people call "white lies" are a sub-category of honorable lying. They're done out of niceness. Such as the time I told Dawn Spurlock she should definitely continue to pursue her knitting projects because she showed great potential in that area. Or, a long-ago girl writing to her soldier brother that everything is just dandy back at home, when to be honest, all the silver-plate has already been looted, and the pigs and chickens carried off to feed the troops.

Other honorable lies are the ones you tell to put a good

face to the world. These lies have something to do with loyalty, which is important to us Hawkinses.

But school lies are a whole different category entirely. I learned all about school lies last year in Colonial History, when I read what our school textbook said compared to the books Mrs. Dooley helped me find in the library, and what I found out reading *American History* magazine, which I subscribe to. Mrs. Dooley helped me get what she called primary sources for the papers I had to write—like letters and diaries and proclamations and so forth. I finally figured out that my schoolbook was propping up some very wobbly ideas. There were all these ugly, unspoken facts swimming around the murky bottom, under the glossy surface pages of our textbook. And then I started to wonder if everybody was telling these kinds of wobbly, propping-up lies all the time, all around me.

If maybe they slid by so smoothly, I just never realized, even when I was bobbing like a cork in an ocean of falsehoods.

CHAPTER ONE

My grandma Lady is chock-full of opinions that tend to kink up the best-laid plans. I always knew Lady was a fusspot who drove a hard bargain, but it never really sunk in until we had to go live with her.

For example, six days after we move in with Lady and Grandpa Tad, me and Daddy are planning a road trip to Cherokee, North Carolina. We aim to go to the funeral of Daddy's buddy Trilby Bigwitch, who fought with Daddy's army unit in Vietnam.

Lady has one thing to say about this plan, and then she has another, and then another thing on top.

"You're hardly even unpacked yet from moving in," she says.

"You need to prepare for school starting Monday," she says.

To tell the truth, I do not need to prepare for school; the whole idea of seventh grade is dreadful. I'm trying every trick I can dream up not to dwell on it. Though, she's right—I haven't technically unpacked any boxes. I did carry them up to the second floor. I did stack them in a corner of what is supposed to be my depressing bedroom, down the hall from Daddy's depressing bedroom and the smaller room Ma sleeps in.

My so-called bedroom has purple floral wallpaper and a polished secretary desk with claw feet like a monster. It has a fireplace that looks like it hasn't been lit for two hundred years. Clear as day, no child has ever inhabited that room. I don't see why I have to be the courageous pioneer.

Lady and Tad's farmhouse is only eight miles away from my real home, and it's still inside the town boundaries of Love's Forge, but it might as well be a million. It is a place that creaks if you put a toe down on any floorboard. It has wood shutters that bang in the slightest breath of wind. It has a musty parlor that attracts damp and that nobody sits in except after supper. It has a kitchen full of Tennessee knickknacks, including two framed needlepoint pictures.

The first one says: *Blood makes you related. Loyalty makes you family.*

The second one says: *In Time of Test, Family Is Best*.

Which I agree with one hundred percent. Only I would add:

A Family of Three
Was Plenty for Me.

Lady and Grandpa Tad's house does come with an over-grown, weedy garden, which Ma could grow her gargantuan root vegetables in, if she ever has a mind to get out of bed again. But if any ponies or goats or chickens ever inhabited the barn or coop, my grandma Lady has long since run them off.

What I want most is to be back in our cottage where I was born, only us three, with the doghouse in the backyard, and the birdhouse by my window, and the playhouse in the walnut tree, all matching with white clapboard and shingle roofs. Daddy and I built all those little homes to look ex-actly like the sweet life-sized home we used to live in.

What I want second most, even though I am not partial to funerals, is to go on this road trip with Daddy. When you take a perfect road trip, you go somewhere you've never been before, and then you circle back to where you started out, and it makes you feel both adventurous and cozy.

But here we are on Friday afternoon in my grandma Lady's kitchen, the hot air positively swimming with Lady's opinions. She is objecting up one side and down the other to me going along to Trilby's service with Daddy.

"It's inappropriate, taking an eleven-year-old girl to be around all those rough men at a military funeral," Lady says.

Inappropriate is one of Lady's favorite words. It's a word meant to shave the square edges off a person.

She adds, "You don't know the first thing about raising girls to become young ladies, son."

Daddy and Ma raised me up fine so far, I think. *Without all of your opinions.*

"I need Lyndie in the passenger seat to read road signs," Daddy argues. "I'll be concentrating on navigating the hair-pin turns."

It's hardly even a two-hour trip to Cherokee, but Smoky Mountain roads are full of devilish curves, with sick-making drops alongside, so it pays to look sharp. Because Daddy is half-blind in his left eye thanks to a flying piece of shrap-nel, and always drives over the speed limit, he needs me to copilot, and I am proud to do it. I'm standing behind his chair, and I put my chin on his shoulder and look down at the road map spread out on the kitchen table. That curvy, curly road from Love's Forge to Cherokee, North Carolina, is a challenge I can handle.

"As a bonus," Daddy says. "If there's trouble, I can always count on Lyndon Baines Hawkins to fast-talk our way out of it, right Lyndie? She takes after her namesake that way." He means old president Lyndon Johnson, who I was named for, and who was famous for his powers of persuasion.

I give Daddy a good kick under his chair. "There won't *be* any trouble!"

"Tyrus Hawkins." Lady is polishing my school loafers—she waves one at the map. "Correct me if I'm wrong, but it's a single road through the mountains. You'd have to drive blindfolded and seated backward to get lost. You don't need Lyndie's help with this."

"Point." Daddy swivels his head around at me. "As your grandpa Tad would say: Counterpoint?"

Grandpa Tad is a lawyer; nobody can beat him in an argument. I'm thrilled he isn't here to take Lady's side.

"The thing is," I blurt out, "I *have* to go." Even I can hear how raw and true those words sound.

Lady looks up sharply. She sets one polished loafer on a square of frayed towel and stares first at me, then at my father. "And why would that be?"

I can't tell Lady I only yesterday found a half-full bottle of George Dickel Tennessee Whisky in Daddy's car's glove box. Lady is big on personal privacy—that is, when it comes to her own privacy. She doesn't approve of children

7

snooping in glove boxes, or in dresser drawers, or any-where else either, so I'm in a pickle. A kid only gets to find out important stuff "on a need to know basis," according to my grandmother.

Lady strictly doesn't approve of liquor. Who knows what kind of lockdown she would put us all under, if she found out Daddy was secret-keeping whiskey? I'd probably never get to take another car ride with Daddy again in my life. I have chosen to accept my mission: to keep Lady's nose as far out of our business as I can manage and make sure Daddy gets home safe.

"The old Hawkins homestead," I croak out, drumming up a good lie. I give Daddy another kick with my foot. "We want to stop in Greeneville on our way back, to visit where Grandpa Tad's granddaddy grew up."

"Right!" Daddy picks up the thread with enthusiasm. He's improvisational like that. "Lyndie's been pestering me about the old homestead."

"I haven't seen that place since I was nine," I add. "I want to make a diagram of the eighteenth-century barn. And the many log outbuildings."

There isn't a drop of truth in this, but there *could be,* and Lady knows it. Here is the one and only thing me and my grandma share in common—an appreciation for local history. Although I will say, we do disagree hotly on many of the historical particulars.

"That's the most sensible thing I've heard," Lady says. "Your grandpa's grandfather Fayette Hawkins lived and died right here." Lady taps her finger on the map and lifts her chin at Daddy. "And your grandpa spent many a summer there. Maybe some of Fayette's unimpeachable character and high dignity will rub off on your daughter."

"I believe that might happen," Daddy says.

"I suppose if you'll be in Cherokee, you could visit your sister in Bryson City," she suggests. She means my aunt Palm Rae. We don't see much of her because her husband is mayor, and "a very busy man."

"We could look into that," Daddy says.

"And what does Lyndie's mother say?" Lady asks.

Lady knows Ma has no opinion how I come or go. Ma started having headaches last spring when Daddy was let go from his work. They've gotten worse since we moved in with Lady and Grandpa Tad. Ma has already relocated from the parents' room into a smaller room down the hall. When she's not at her new job at Miller's Department Store, she stays holed up in that room chewing on Bayer aspirins.

Lady is stalling, conjuring up one last objection. A shimmer of doubt passes through her ice-blue eyes.

"Mama," Daddy says. "We'll be all right."

Say yes, I pray silently. *Please.*

If Lady wins this battle, how will I fight her on the next?

It feels like forever before Lady sighs and her shoulders relax a notch. "I don't like this a bit."

"Duly noted," Daddy says. "We appreciate your concern."

I want to throw victory air-punches. But I am doing my best to look unimpeachable and dignified, like old Fayette Hawkins.

"You head right home after, you hear me, son? You leave tomorrow morning. I want you back before the sun sets." Lady points to her wall calendar. "Back the *same day.* Saturday, September 7, 1985," she says meaningfully to Daddy, enunciating all the numbers. "Lyndie needs to unpack her school clothes and get settled in."

"Yes, ma'am!" Daddy barks. He offers me his pinky finger. We shake on our victory. And I feel my whole insides beginning to unfurl.

Holy Hallelujah! Me and Daddy together again in his El Camino, aka the Blue Bullet! Come tomorrow, we'll be heading down the wide-open road to Freedom From Lady.

"Promise me," Lady says. "You'll get home before dark."

"Okay, okay, okay," I say. "We'll be home before dark. We promise."

CHAPTER TWO

Last March, Daddy lost his job shimmying up and down electric poles with the Tennessee Valley Authority.

"He's got the flu," Ma told me, when Daddy didn't get dressed and go off to work six days running. Me and Ma were in the garden behind our cottage one Saturday, pulling the last of the winter vegetables out of the hard ground and tossing them into a basket.

"Daddy doesn't look one bit fluish to me." I nudged our bluetick hound dog, Hoopdee, away with one foot, so I could get a good grip on what I thought might be a kohlrabi. Or maybe a rutabaga. Hoopdee was mostly still a big puppy then. He was clawing giant holes in the dirt to help us dig, with a lot more enthusiasm than precision.

Hoopdee had perfectly good islands of smooth gray fur

floating between naked oceans of pink-and-black-speckled skin. He'd been nose-to-tail mangy when Daddy found him meandering across four lanes of downtown traffic. Daddy showed me how to rub him down with apple cider vinegar to fix the mange, and I did, but Hoopdee was still in recovery.

"I'm a genius," Ma cried. She held up a pale, double-footed root nearly as long as her hand. "Lookee what I grew."

Ma always said root vegetables were her favorite, because the good part was hidden underground, like a secret, until you pulled it up.

"I would be impressed," I said, "if I was an extended family of gourmet rabbits."

Ma stood up straight and gazed at me. "This is an icicle radish." She brushed a bit of dirt off it. "I loved vegetables at your age."

"That's 'cause Grandma and Grandpa were hippies," I said. "You had no choice about vegetables—the weirder, the better. At least they named you and Auntie Pearl Rainbow and Pearl, instead of Rutabaga and Parsnip."

"I don't know, Parsnip would be a snappy name. I wish I'd thought of that for *you*."

"Please stop changing my subject. Why is Daddy home?"

Ma tucked a tendril of blond hair back into her bandana. She regarded me evenly. "What?"

"Daddy is not sick, unless being ravenous is a disease. He ate every one of my Hostess cherry pies in the pantry yesterday, plus half a box of Lucky Charms. Although it's true, he does smell funny."

"Funny how?"

"Sweet and sour," I said. "Like old fruit."

Ma's smile froze. "Must be all those cherry pies." I caught a glint of impatient anger in her eyes before she bent back to pulling vegetables, her skinny rump in her paisley skirt turned to me.

"Ma?" I whined. "Why is Daddy home all the time?"

"Oh, Lyndie!" she barked over her shoulder. "Your dad was let go by the TVA."

"Let go? But he's had that job fixing electric lines since forever!"

I waited for her to explain, but she kept fishing up radishes and parsnips and Jerusalem artichokes, fast now, one after another, and tossing them into her basket.

"Are you mad he got let go? That's not his fault, is it?"

"Fault?" Ma said. "Fault?" Clods of dirt flew up around her where she and Hoopdee were digging furiously side by side. "If I could untangle the reasons, for good and bad, why people do what they do in this world, I would be a woman at peace."

Daddy stayed upstairs for two weeks; that's when I first heard him pacing. *Clack, clack, clack* went his boots on the floorboards every hour of the night and day. I saw him ghost into the bathroom now and then, trailing his sour smell. I knew he snuck downstairs when he thought we were sleeping. When I went rummaging for breakfast, I found nothing but crumbs in the Lucky Charms boxes. And Tootsie Pops wrappers scattered on the pantry floor. It was like living in a nest of raccoons, only lots more worrisome.

Then, one day after school, I was up in my room making ink, like the Civil War soldiers did when they wrote letters home. It was Mrs. Dooley down at Love's Forge Library who told me how lonely the soldiers were during that long war, how they went to the trouble to make ink out of berries to write their families, and used feathers or stiff straw for pens. Writing home helped the soldiers keep up their spirits, Mrs. Dooley said.

I mashed up a cup of raspberries and two tablespoons of vinegar in a bowl with the back of a spoon and scissored a pointed end on a crow feather from Ma's vegetable garden. I was imagining how it felt to be a frostbitten, exhausted, starving, homesick soldier, missing his beloved sister with all his heart. "My Dearest Annie," I wrote, smudgily, but with lots of attractive watery pink flourishes, at the top of the paper. "I trust this letter finds you well . . ."

I was dipping my quill pen back in the berry ink when I heard the crash and tinkle of glass breaking downstairs.

It wasn't only one crash, either. It was a *crash,* pause, *crash,* pause, *crash,* pause.

I threw down my quill pen and jumped to my feet.

Daddy opened his bedroom door right as I was slipping downstairs on tiptoe. His face was rigid, he'd heard too, and I knew strange sounds always scared him. When he saw me, he backed away into his room. I could tell the smashing was coming from the kitchen. When I ran downstairs and peeked around the doorjamb, I saw Ma.

She was standing at our kitchen window in her pajamas with a ballpeen hammer in one fist. Each and every one of the little panes of glass in the window had been broken, one by one, deliberately.

"Ma!" I cried. "Why are you bashing out our windows?" Ma's face was white with fury when she spun around, but her expression crumpled soon as she saw me.

"You'd better ask your father why," she said. She set the ballpeen hammer carefully on the kitchen table. "I'm going for a walk," she said. "You stay."

I crept back upstairs. Daddy's door was closed, and

though I knocked softly, he grunted and yelled in a muffled voice, "Go away!" It didn't seem like a good time to ask him why Ma was smashing windows.

I watched from my bedroom window while Ma marched down our driveway wearing rain boots and plaid pajamas under her winter coat, her scarf fluttering behind her in the wind. When she'd marched out of sight, I took up my quill pen again.

But my writing was illegible and blotchy now, and the whole idea of letters from homesick soldiers to waiting, anxious sisters made me so sad, all I could do was sit on the floor gasping. I'd never seen Ma do anything even halfway so confounding as to bash out those windows. She was a born and bred peacenik from a whole family of peaceniks and raised on a commune with four other families, in harmony and goodwill. Ma didn't believe in swatting flies.

Plus, if Ma and Daddy had ever said a harsh word to each other, I hadn't heard it. But that night, when I lay awake in bed, I heard plenty of harsh words. There was a freak ice storm outside, and Ma's angry, accusing voice rose above the sleet that tapped at our windows. And underneath it all in a steady rhythm, Daddy talked low and soothing. I mashed my ear hard to my bedroom door and tried to will away the whistling wind and patter of ice, to make out what topic they were fighting over. "You are a disappointed man," I heard Ma yell. Or did she say *disappointing*? I'm not sure of the word, only the emotion of it. But the two words I did hear clear, over and over, were *promise me.* *Promise me.*

Next morning, Daddy came down early in a pressed shirt and smelling less like sour apples and more like Aqua Velva aftershave lotion. Every day after that, he went out, asking up and down Love's Forge and Gatlinburg and even as far as Knoxville for work. Afternoons, when he got home, the sharp crease in his slacks had gone flat and his work application papers, telling about who he was and all the marvelous things he could do, were crumpled and folded all which way. Pretty soon there were no more boxes of Lucky Charms cereal in our pantry, much less any Hostess cherry pies.

Then, after two weeks, Ma marched out again and came back with a job at Miller's Department Store selling foundation garments. It paid "a pittance," and she had to have lots of sincere discussions about hosiery, girdles, and underwear. Ma looked older and more tired in her Miller's uniform. It kind of made me sad that when she was younger her and her friends took off their bras and set them on fire to stand up for women's rights. Now she was selling brassieres to rich old ladies. She had to work from afternoon until eight o'clock most nights.

By then, except for Hoopdee practicing his baying, *whoooooarrrrr, yo, yo, yooooo,* our house had gone full silent. Once or twice, sitting at breakfast, I saw Daddy try to touch Ma's hand, but she quick grabbed her juice glass, or pulled her fingers out of reach. Seeing her do that was like watching loneliness take shape from thin air.

Packing my things to move into Lady and Grandpa Tad's house, it felt super important to organize all my stuff in the exact right-size boxes, with handwritten labels, and plenty of tape. Especially the arrowheads and antique shell casings and other historical paraphernalia I'd been collecting on our road trips. I was going to offer them to the Love's Forge History Museum soon as I had a highly significant collection, and I didn't want anything to get lost.

On our last day, there was still plenty to do. I had all my history books in one pile and the overdue Civil War library books for Mrs. Dooley in another. I couldn't help looking at those books one last time before I put them in a box. I got sucked in, reading about Abraham Lincoln. I think I would have liked old Abraham, who was a lawyer, like Grandpa

Tad. There was something about his eyes looking out from his photographic portraits. I pictured sitting with him by the fire in the shabby White House on a threadbare rug—just me and Mr. Lincoln and his bodyguard William H. Johnson, who was his best friend, listening to the president read his first draft of the Gettysburg Address, him stopping to cross out a line or add one, until he got the words to match how he was hearing them in his heart.

Ma poked in six, seven, eight times to check on me. "The clock is ticking, Lyndie," she said. "Please finish your packing." On the ninth time, she marched in and started throwing stuff into random boxes.

"For goodness' sake, Ma!" I yelled. "You can't put Hoopdee's doggy blanket in the same box with maps and clothes and postcards. Stop it. You're mixing everything up."

"You can sort it out when we get to your grandparents' house," Ma said, exasperated. "It's time we got out of here. Please, Lyndie. My head is killing me."

"We can't just *get out* of some place I spent my whole life since I was a tiny infant!" I cried.

"I'm sorry, baby," Ma said. "There's nothing else to do. We closed on the house day before yesterday. Mr. Grubecker is moving in this afternoon."

"Will we buy our house back after Daddy finds work?"

Ma didn't answer as Daddy came in and took the boxes.

I trudged outside, still fuming, and stuffed everything I could carry into the flatbed of Daddy's Blue Bullet, between Ma's gardening supplies and my precious boxes of collectibles. Daddy threw a tarp over everything and started putting on bungee cords. His hands were shaking so bad, he could hardly fix the cords.

I opened my mouth to ask him why his hands were jumping around like that, but the look on his face made me change my mind. I watched while he went back to the house and locked our front door. He fumbled the key under a flowerpot. Like we were going on vacation. Like we'd be back and unpacking our suitcases before Wally Grubecker had the first chance to move his leatherette La-Z-Boy recliner into our living room.

Then we stuffed ourselves into the Blue Bullet. Ma insisted on driving—good thing, since I doubt Daddy could have held a steering wheel with those jumpy hands. I craned around one last time to see out the back window when we drove off. Between all the boxes and suitcases on the flatbed I could glimpse our cottage, and the little matching dog- and bird- and kid-houses, getting smaller and vaguer.

Babe, they say your ears are long, I sang softly to Hoopdee, to the tune of Sonny and Cher, trying to calm myself down and calm Hoopdee down too. He was sliding around in great agitation on my lap between Ma and Daddy in the front seat. He usually rode in the flatbed and that was his preference. *I got you, babe,* I whispered. Hoopdee's neck fur smelled like warm bread baked by a bear.

And I still had Ma and Daddy, sort of, even if they had gone nearly full silent on each other. They were not on the same side anymore. I was really hoping my parents would hurry up and sign a peace treaty.

I decided I would not let them sit in awkward wordlessness for the whole darn drive. "When you find a new job, can we buy our house back from Mr. Grubecker?" I sat up and asked Daddy.

"I don't know about that," Daddy said. "But I promise someday you and me will build a better house, with all the mod cons."

"Better start keeping one promise at a time," Ma said, her eyes steady on the road.

"I don't want a better house," I said. "I don't want any mod cons."

"We'll be closer to school now," Daddy said.

"Seven miles closer to Covenant Academy," I said peevishly. "I feel so blessed. And nine miles farther away from the library and Mrs. Dooley. What a great deal." After Daddy and Ma and Dawn Spurlock, Mrs. Dooley the librarian was pretty much my favorite person in the known universe.

"You can hold the sarcasm, Lyndon Baines," Ma said.

"Grandpa and Grandma's house is not far uphill from Spurlocks'," Daddy said. He was still twitchy, but I could tell he was trying hard to be still. "You and Dawn Spurlock can run up and down to see each other all the time now."

Dawn is my only true and best friend. I'd hardly laid eyes on her for half the summer, with all our packing and moving rigmarole.

"Maybe the Tennessee Valley Authority will give you your job back," I said. Daddy's mouth turned down, and his hands trembled in his lap. He clenched them tighter.

"What's wrong with your hands?" I said.

"Ah," Daddy said. "Just nerves, punkin'."

"Jobs don't find themselves." Ma blew a long breath through her lips and let up on the gas to take a curve. "You don't look, you don't get hired." Ma fished a Kleenex out of her purse between us. Her eyes were glistening. That made my heart soften a little. I was sorry I yelled at her about packing my boxes.

"Do you still feel headachy?" I put my cheek against her arm, which was smooth and powdery.

"Yes." Ma was taking deep breaths. "But I'm okay."

I looked at Daddy, then at Ma, and for the first time ever in my life, I thought, *I don't think my parents know how to head us in the right direction.* We were driving straight down the highway into a future I did not want and never agreed to.

CHAPTER THREE

A full twenty-four hours after the time I promised Lady we'd be home from Trilby Bigwitch's funeral, me and Daddy are pulling in past the American flag tied to the gate at the end of Lady and Grandpa Tad's driveway. It's late Sunday afternoon.

A police car sits parked out front. Lady stands talking to two officers, a woman and her skinny partner. The air is electric with the crackle of walkie-talkies. Grandpa Tad has one leg in the cab of his truck, and Hoopdee is circling and bawling. Mr. Spurlock, Dawn's dad, is there, and so is Dawn.

Dawn gets to me first and about yanks me through the open window of Daddy's Blue Bullet. "You're going to be grounded until pigs quit oinking," she says, hugging me tight. She smells like rose soap. "But school starts tomorrow, so we'll see each other all the time anyway."

Dawn has on a sweater vest she's knitted, with armholes askew and a neckline that looks like hamsters gnawed on it. She's been practice-knitting for months. I admire her grim persistence in the face of repeated failures.

Daddy gets out of the car and strides over to talk to Lady and the police and Grandpa Tad. The conversation looks like it might turn explosive.

I climb out too. "How mad are they?" I put one hand on my hip and cut my eyes at Lady.

"I think they might be somewhat upset?" Dawn says. "I definitely heard the words *missing persons report*?"

"Oh, hell's bells," I say. "Did you hear the word *APB*?"

"I don't think *APB* is technically a word," Dawn says.

I sigh. "Did you hear the phrase *All-Points Bulletin*?"

"There was a lot of police radio talk," Dawn says. "I didn't catch the exact sense. Just the general tone." She adds brightly, "I don't believe Hoopdee is at all mad at you, though."

"So you're saying, one-sixth of the Hawkins clan doesn't want to kill me." Dawn cocks one eyebrow. She never laughs at my jokes.

"Guess what else?" she says. "We're getting a boy to

come live with us for the whole school year. From a juvenile detention center." She looks smug as a bug. "He's a criminal, and we are going to rehabilitate him."

Dawn's family is big on charity projects. But the care and feeding of juvenile delinquent criminals has never come up before. "Hoo-boy," I say. "Aren't you worried? He could steal your jewelry. Empty your bank accounts. Or poison your whole family with strychnine-laced waffles. What if he pummels your little brothers on an ongoing basis?"

"That stuff only happens in movies, Lyndie. Not in Love's Forge."

But now the grown-ups rush over and Grandpa Tad swallows us up with his angry, anxious questions. He glares at me over his horn-rimmed glasses. Am I in one piece? Well, thank heavens for that. And why couldn't I find myself a dad-gummed phone booth and dial home? Didn't I think my grandmother's peace of mind was worth the twenty-five cents it would cost me?

My grandmother's peace of mind? Without me there, Daddy might have been driving along those curvy roads tipsy and half-blind. She is *lucky* I was with him the whole time. I don't say any of that.

Lady stands over me with her white hair in a perfect up-do and her lipsticked mouth set in a line that's a lot more formidable than Grandpa Tad's yelling about the price of a Bell Telephone call.

"How was I to know you all weren't tumped over in a ditch?" she snaps. "Or something worse?"

"I'm sorry, Lady," I say. "We got lost, and, well."

"Enough." Lady freezes me with one look. "Sorry is as sorry does. School starts tomorrow. Get inside and organize your school clothes. We'll hash this out soon enough, you'd better believe it."

She marches me inside. So I don't get to hear any more about the criminal boy coming to live with Dawn.

I don't get to tell Dawn I met my first real dead person, either, at the Longhouse Funeral Home in Cherokee, North Carolina.

It didn't throw me much, least, not at first. I have a pretty strong tolerance for grossness, on account of all the research I've conducted on the Civil War, where soldiers had rotten feet and amputated limbs and scurvy, and sometimes got left dying on the battlefield to be eaten by hogs. This particular dead soldier in his coffin, he was a fine picture in comparison to those Union and Confederate corpses: Trilby Bigwitch wore his dress army uniform and gray cap. The only thing that made it bad in particular was that Trilby was Daddy's buddy, and Daddy got shook up to see him.

Trilby Bigwitch had a face full of parts that had nothing in common—a nose like the prow of a ship, a hairline that darted down into his forehead like it had somewhere to get to. He had a gold earring in one ear.

Looking down into Trilby's coffin, Daddy folded his hands, took a long breath, and said, "Trilby, buddy. You broke our deal. You saved my life. I was supposed to save yours. Remember?"

"What deal?" I whispered. "He saved your life?" Daddy shrugged and turned away.

A man got up to speak the service first in the Cherokee language, second in English, one sentence at a time, back and forth: "It is good to see our cousins here today. It is good to see our brothers and our family here today. We have come to build one fire."

Wow, I thought, craning around. *All these hundred and fifty people are family?* The trumpeter played "Taps," slow and mournful. Daddy and three other soldiers, all in full dress uniform, folded up the American flag into a beautiful triangle, and Daddy presented it to Trilby's wife.

Behind me in a pew, a lady said quietly, "That woman

has had sorrow piled on top of sorrow. To have her husband do such a terrible thing. It's more trouble than anybody deserves."

"Well, bless him, Trilby is free now. He's out of pain," said her neighbor.

"He'll be going to a better home."

What terrible thing did he do? What pain was he in? How is he free? The conversation reminded me of our school textbooks, skimming over the glossy surface.

"We should go back to Lady's house now," I told Daddy after the service. I had a million questions I needed answers for.

"Not yet," Daddy said. "There's a wake."

I didn't know why you'd have a *wake* for a person who would never be woken again.

"People used to stay awake all night," Daddy explained. "Keeping watch over the body." Reading my thoughts. He does that sometimes.

The wake was in another room of the funeral home. I went over and told Mrs. Bigwitch I was really sorry about Trilby. "I never met him," I said. "But Daddy thought the world of him. Daddy wished he had kept in better touch with Trilby." Mrs. Bigwitch tried to smile, but her smile came out upside down and her eyes went shiny. I wondered about what other sorrows she'd had piling up. She looked so kindly.

After a while, I pulled on Daddy's sleeve again. "It's going on dark, Daddy." We said good-bye to Mrs. Bigwitch and climbed back into the Blue Bullet. "This map says we need to go northwest to get back to Love's Forge."

"Not just yet," Daddy said.

The horizon went yellow, then gold, then red, and then purple. I handed Daddy his glasses with the one thick lens to correct his half-blind eye. *We promise!* I heard myself telling Lady. *We'll be home before dark.* I wedged my knees against the glove box in case Daddy had any mind to feel around in there for his whiskey bottle. We drove until both my feet were asleep. After a while, I dozed off.

It was three a.m. by the lit clock on the dashboard when I woke up with a start.

"Trilby wrote poems," Daddy said out of nowhere. It felt like he'd been talking for a while, and I'd dropped into the middle of his conversation.

"What?" My feet had fallen asleep again, and I was groggy. "The speed limit is forty-five on this road," I reminded him.

"One poem of Trilby's I remember." Daddy let up on the gas and rubbed a hand over his chin. "It tells about a wounded soldier who flies home. But when he gets to his house, there's nothing there. Where his house is supposed to be there's nothing but a big dark hole in the ground."

Daddy made a sound of pain deep in his chest.

The streetlamps we passed under lit up his face and the curly tips of his shaggy red hair and the wetness on his cheeks. Light and dark. Light and dark.

I pictured the poem-soldier in his pressed army uniform decorated with bravery medals, maybe on crutches because his leg was shot up, staring into the dark hole where his home should be. I wondered if our real home, when we drove away from it last week, sank into the earth and disappeared too.

When the sun poked between the trees in the morning, Daddy pulled over in a drugstore parking lot, and I went to find a bathroom and buy some Big League Chew Gumballs, which are our favorite. I thought a gumball might cheer Daddy up. We pushed our car seats back and looked up through the windshield at the clouds.

I blew a grape-flavored bubble. "I just want to know one thing about why you and Trilby were in Vietnam."

Daddy fumbled with a tissue, wiped his face.

"What was the whole point?" I passed him another gumball.

"Oh, I don't know. You know about our American Civil War, right?" Daddy asked between chews.

"Don't play dumb. I'm a bottomless pit of trivia on the Civil War, and you know it." This was thanks in part to many road trips Daddy and I took to history exhibits and museums and stores selling memorabilia all over South Carolina and Tennessee and Georgia and Mississippi.

"Vietnam was a civil war," Daddy said. "Only, it was already split into two separate countries. The North country, the communists, wanted to unify back up with the South country."

"Did Vietnamese families split down the middle and fight on opposite sides? Like during our Civil War?"

"Yes," Daddy said. "They surely did."

I always steered clear of studying too much on the Vietnam War. I learned not to ask questions about it by the time I was in first grade. There was a big bothersome silence around it—that war was like a house hole, something that used to be there but then vanished, sucked underground.

I hardly ever heard anything about Vietnam in all the time I was growing up. But once when I was a little kid, I was spending the night with Lady and Grandpa Tad, supposed to be well up in bed, but as usual, I was not tired and spying from the stairwell. On the phone in the kitchen,

Lady was talking to my aunt Palm Rae. She said, after the war, Daddy "came home a little bit different." *Different how?* I wondered. *What was he like before?*

After a while, Daddy spit his gum into the ashtray. "Guys like Trilby ought never to have been over there," he said. "Trilby had too much heart to be killing people and having enemies."

"But what about guys like you?" I said. "Don't you have a big heart like Trilby did?"

Daddy glanced at me; it was a quick, lit-up look, like he'd been shocked wide-awake. "Maybe I did," he said. "Once."

I knew we were disobeying Lady, and surely looking at a heap of trouble when we finally landed back in Love's Forge. But it felt most important to be exactly where we were. Right there at that moment. We were figuring out things Daddy needed to know.

CHAPTER FOUR

Monday morning. First day of seventh grade. I'm standing in Lady and Grandpa Tad's hallway, alone, in my stiff,
spotless blazer and ironed pleated skirt and polished loafers,
holding my new divider notebooks Lady bought me.

Ma's still asleep; she got home late from selling girdles
last night. Daddy's awake—I know because I hear his footsteps pacing upstairs in his bedroom, but he didn't answer
when I knocked earlier. When Lady hustles out from the
kitchen, she's sewn up the broken strap on my book bag.
She hands it to me at the door, gives me a look up and
down, and flicks a piece of lint off my blazer collar. "You be
your best self today."

I don't think Lady's idea of *best self* and my idea are an
exact match. It's seven o'clock in the morning, but Lady is

already fully gussied up in a pink pantsuit, her white hair teased into a beehive, and her lipstick on, lipstick the exact pink color of the pantsuit.

"No sassing your teachers, Lyndie. And you come straight home. You know why?"

"Because I'm grounded until next week," I say.

"You know what for?"

"For staying away all night with Daddy, and not even phoning to say we were safe."

"You're old enough to know how to dial a phone," Lady says, as if she hasn't made this observation a hundred times since yesterday.

"Daddy needed to talk."

"Don't you worry your head about your daddy. He's in his own kind of hot water."

Of course he is, because if Lady has her way, nobody will ever put a foot down to the right or left without her say-so.

Clack, clack, clack go Daddy's boots on the floorboards above us. Lady raises her eyes to the ceiling. When she looks back at me, two worry lines have appeared on her forehead.

"You head right home once school lets out and unpack your boxes."

I scuffle a loafer on the wood floor. I'm not going to unpack my boxes ever. "I hate school," I say. "Nobody likes me."

"Don't be ridiculous," Lady says. "Dawn Spurlock likes you fine."

I've been at Covenant Baptist Academy since third grade. Even being best friends with Dawn, who is the world's eternal optimist, can't turn the sow's ear of Covenant into a silk purse. I got moved from the public school to Covenant because Lady argued I needed to go to school with all the "nice" girls in Love's Forge. Ma didn't like it. She said under her breath that Covenant was full of "Deep South snobs and religious wackos." But she'd stopped *speaking truth to power* by then. She went along to get along with Lady. Grandpa Tad pays my tuition.

"I hate it," I say again.

"Too bad," Lady says. "Eleven-year-old girls go to school. That's a hard fact of life. It's a five-minute walk. Go on downhill through Spurlocks' yard until you meet the main road, then turn left. Hurry up now so you can catch Dawn. You're already late."

"Where's Grandpa Tad?"

Lady propels me out the door. "Tad went to the law office. I'll be at the museum most all day, giving tours." Lady is Chairwoman of the Board at Love's Forge History Museum. I've been on tours with her before, and no kidding, she does have a wealth of factual knowledge.

"But who will watch out for Ma and Daddy?"

Lady hesitates a fraction. She gives me a curious look, then says firmly, "Your mama and daddy are two grown people, Lyndie. They don't need you watching out for them. Seems to me, you have more than enough to keep you busy, watching out for *yourself*. Enough, now. Get a move on."

I meander down the walkway and turn left across the lawn to take the shortcut to Dawn's house. Before I round the side of the barn, I glance back at Lady and Grandpa Tad's farmhouse. Lady is on the porch with her arms crossed. She uncrosses and points down the hill.

I have never been grounded before. Being grounded could put a serious crimp in my freedom. Back at home, I could stay up watching TV till I felt sleepy. Lady's house has no TV. I could bike down to the library on a whim. Now the library is too far away. I could eat Lucky Charms cereal out of the box in bed. Lady doesn't keep sugary cereal in the house.

At our house, I never had to pick up my room. If I wanted to draw maps on my walls, I could do that. I have a notion Lady would not look kindly on diagrams of the battles of Antietam and Gettysburg chalked up on her wallpaper. But one thing I know from studying the Union and Confederate generals, when it comes to winning in battle, you have to know how to bluff. You set up tricky diversions. And if things don't go like you hoped, you should *always* have an escape plan.

When Hoopdee gets sight of me, he unravels himself from the barn shadows and gives me a gigantic yawn with his pink tongue flicking. He scrambles to his feet and comes galumphing after me downhill, his panting breath tickling my legs. I squat down and gather his whole wriggling body into my arms. "Did you freeze your paws in the barn last night?"

Hoopdee can't sleep on my bed now, because Lady dislikes him in the house. Daddy did sneak him up for me the night we moved in, but Lady found little gray hairs all over and smelled what she called a "houndy odor," and boy, was she hot about it. Now there's an empty spot in my bed where Hoopdee belongs.

The trail down to Spurlocks' winds through a mess of trees. My feet slow, and slow, and slow. I'm late for real now. My plaid skirt itches. My blazer is an inferno. Already my knee socks have drooped round my ankles. I feel rubbed wrong every which way.

I wander off the path, sideways, not toward Dawn's house and not toward school, thinking I'll look to see if there might be some blackberries left. I do find a few bushes, but it's too late for fruit; the birds have gobbled the bushes clean. I manage to scratch up my hands digging around in the brambles.

Hoopdee trots off, nosing farther into the trees. The air feels thin and bright. And then I hear Hoopdee start his baying, *whooooooarrrrr, yo. Whoooooarrrr, yo, yo.*

"Oh heck," I whisper, and start running for him. If Lady hears and puts two and two together, she could guess where I am. Not even halfway near school.

I find Hoopdee about fifteen yards down the path. When I rush up on him, I see what he's caterwauling about.

"Oh, Hoopdee!" I cry out. "Leave off!" I grab him by the scruff and haul him backward. "Sit now, and hush up." He does drop halfway down on his haunches, quivering, indignant with me. "All the way down!" I insist. Reluctantly, he lowers to a crouch.

The little deer is lying in some brush near the path with three of its legs tucked and its neck stretched out like I've seen puppies do. It has black tips on its ears, and it is old enough that its white spots are starting to get covered with new tan winter fur. But it's still gangly, mostly big brown eyeballs and a sensitive black nose. It seems too tired to even pay attention to Hoopdee. I step up to it quietly, hardly daring to breathe.

Something's wrong with one of its front legs. Maybe some animal bit it, or it scraped its shin and got infected. It's torn open from hoof to knee, a big gash with the blood dried dark around the wound, but still raw. No way could it get around on that.

The little deer sighs when my shadow falls over it. I drop my book bag and crouch down, not touching it and keeping still, till it gets used to me—and then I ever so carefully pet the suede-colored back. It's wet with morning dew. "Where's your mama?" I ask. "Did she run off and leave you?" The fawn twitches its damp fur under my hand. It must have been here all night. No mama deer would leave it like that.

"All right," I say. "You're all right. I won't leave you alone, I promise."

The deer has sweet, grassy breath. "We have to wait a bit," I tell it. "Until my grandma goes to her museum. Then we'll get you somewhere safe." I wave at Hoopdee. "Go back now!" I order him. He is budge-less. He lies down and turns his head partway, rolling his eye at me.

I sit cross-legged there for a while, petting the fawn and talking to it, until finally I hear Lady's Cadillac churn down the gravel driveway and purr away along the high ridge road. When Lady's motor falls away to silence, I slide my arms under the fawn's belly, careful not to touch its wounded leg, and pull it close.

It's pretty heavy, but I can lift it okay, even though it gives a half-hearted shiver. It tucks its nose into my armpit, and I carry it slowly back uphill with Hoopdee running ahead, stopping every now and then to set it down and catch my breath, until Lady and Tad's barn appears through the trees.

Lady and Grandpa Tad's barn is filled to the rafters with refrigerators that don't cool, radios that don't broadcast, and fish tanks that won't hold a drop of water, stuff Grandpa has collected from junk sales over the years. But luckily, there's distilled vinegar in Grandpa Tad's tool kit. I clean the fawn's wound with it, careful around the raw part.

I know exactly what to do, because I fixed Hoopdee's mange with vinegar the same way. So long as you can get a good clear look at a wound or a disease, you can fix it. It's the things you can't see, the inside diseases, that are scary.

I hose water into an old hubcap and let the fawn drink. Hoopdee scooches closer to us on his belly, twitching his nose in the air, *huff, huff, huff,* his black ears drooped flat on his neck. "Back you go." I point, and he slouches off a couple of feet. I make the fawn a nest with some old furniture blankets next to a thicket of rusty lawn chairs.

The barn's filtered light and the breeze in the few old hay

bales stirs up a green, outside smell that makes the fawn's eyelids droop. Around noontime, the postman clatters up the road to drop the mail in the box by the gate.

I've got my arm draped around the fawn and my nose close to her twitching ear. She sighs and bundles her head into my neck. I bet I can get her leg healed up in a week, if I keep it clean. She can live in the barn and I'll walk her on a leash every day after school. Maybe I'll take her *to* school, and she can wait patiently outside my homeroom window, which would go some ways to make the school experience bearable.

I guess I fall to sleep thinking about all the things we'll do together, and I'm deep in a dream when I hear a phone ringing and ringing. It goes on, *ring, ring, ring, ring, ring*. When I open my eyes, there's only silence, and Hoopdee licking my nose. I stretch and prop up on one elbow. The sun is much lower outside. Hoopdee snuggles in and puts his muzzle on the fawn's shoulder.

"Your name is Velvet," I tell her, when she blinks her brown eyes at me. Her eyelashes are so long, they brush my cheek. I gently untangle us from each other. Hoopdee lifts his head like to say, *My fawn,* and puts his chin back on Velvet's shoulder.

"I'll sneak into the kitchen for some milk and Quaker

oats. Be right back." I'll have to find out what a fawn is supposed to eat. I bet Mrs. Dooley at the library knows, or can help me find out, if I can figure a way to get over there. I'd better hurry, now. The sun tells me it's got to be near three o'clock.

But as I'm ready to skip for the kitchen, the Blue Bullet pulls into the driveway, with Daddy driving. I guess he dropped off Ma at work. Daddy gets out and walks fast up the drive to get the mail, shoulders tense under his T-shirt. As he's sorting the letters, I can see how fidgety his hands are. On his way back to the house, he stops by the Blue Bullet and fumbles at the car door handle. Glances at the road. He opens the door quick, and ducks into the car.

After a minute, he pulls out of the car and stands upright. I can see clear as day he's got the whiskey bottle. His face in the afternoon sun looks pale and clammy, and now his whole body looks to be jittering. He unscrews the bottle cap, throws back his head, and takes a long, long swig.

Glug, glug, glug. His Adam's apple bobbing.

And as if he swallowed a magic pill, in a snap, all the jittering is gone. His shoulders relax and the lines in his face uncrease. He tilts the bottle to his lips again. When he holds the bottle up to the light, like to judge how much is left, his hands are rock steady.

Now Lady's Cadillac comes purring up the ridge road and turns into the gate. Daddy dives into the car and drops the bottle. He stands back and wipes his mouth on his sleeve. Lady's car door slams and she says something to him. Her high heels crunch on the gravel and tick up the steps, Daddy's heavier boots following. The screen door opens. The screen bangs shut.

All of a sudden, it's like a big magnifying glass in the sky has brought my formerly fuzzy situation into brilliant focus. There are my peeled-off socks, dropped on the barn floor. Beside them, my school blazer is one massive wrinkle. I can see every speck of dust on that blazer, specks that number in the hundreds, maybe in the thousands. There are swipes of blood on my white blouse from my scratched-up hands. And my book bag?

My *book bag*. I dropped my book bag where I found Velvet near the path and completely forgot to pick it up.

With a mushrooming sense of dread, I realize none of this is one bit in line with my desire to get Lady off my case. Not the skipped first day of school. Not the rescued fawn— Lady is definitely not a "friend to all living things." Not the lost book bag, which contains my brand-new notebooks. I suddenly remember Miss Smitty in the front office at Covenant Academy, and her passion for ferreting out tardies and unexcused absences. All afternoon Miss Smitty has been the last thing on my mind. But now?

Now things get even worse in a gigantic way. There are voices in the trees. And here comes Dawn and Mrs. Spurlock scurrying up the path. Dawn is lugging my book bag. Mrs. Spurlock is trotting fast with a covered pie dish in her hands. When they catch sight of Lady's Cadillac in the drive, they pick up their pace and sprint toward the front porch steps. And before I can blink twice, Lady has the screen door open and there is a flurry of conversation on the front porch.

I've got one eye glued to the crack in the barn door. I'm not too far away to get the gist of what's happening. Naturally, Dawn knows I didn't come to school. Naturally, Dawn told her mom, because Dawn tells her mom every little thing. Naturally, they've come up to see about me, wondering am I sick. Naturally, Mrs. Spurlock has brought her famous shoofly pie.

Un-naturally, on the way up, they found my book bag where I dropped it near the path.

And now I see how all the pieces will start to snowball: Lady learns I was not at school. Everyone believes I've gone missing. Maybe dragged away by a woods-prowling bear. Kidnapped by a woods-hiding bandit. Eaten by a woods-dwelling witch.

Behind them, the phone starts to ring. It rings twice and somebody picks up halfway through the third ring. Dawn is holding my book bag in the air like it's evidence from a crime scene. She's hopping from foot to foot, her brown bangs bouncing. Suddenly, my day is looking like a bigger disaster than I imagined it ever could be. If I don't clear up the mystery of my whereabouts in one big hurry, we're going to have the entire Love's Forge police force in Lady and Grandpa Tad's driveway.

Dawn would say: "Do the right thing. You know what that is."

Dawn would say: "Honesty is the best policy."

I guess it's worth a shot. I push open the barn door and step into the sunlight.

CHAPTER FIVE

When Lady and Mrs. Spurlock and Dawn catch sight of me at the barn door, all three mouths drop open. Then Dawn throws down my book bag and jumps up high with outstretched arms, like she's flying. Mrs. Spurlock, in contrast, succumbs to gravity. She plops down hard on the porch swing, still holding her pie plate, and threatens to keel over sideways.

"Sweet heaven above!" Lady cries out. Her double chin trembles, and she swipes the back of her hand across her forehead. But she's also quickest to get a grip on herself and march down the porch steps. Dawn comes scooting after her. Mrs. Spurlock hoists up from the swing and wobbles down the steps, still holding her pie. Then here comes Daddy too, clomping out the screen door, stone-faced.

The whole gaggle of them comes up on me so quick, I don't have time to organize my story.

Lady says, "I'm certain you have an explanation, and I can't *wait* to hear it."

Dawn says, "Lyndie! I knew you'd be totally fine. I told Mama you were fine . . ."

Mrs. Spurlock comes third. She says, in a faint voice, "I brought up a pie."

"Lyndie!" Daddy barks at me. "What in Sam Hill are you doing in there?" Daddy has always been indulgent of me. But skipping school is not on his list of indulgences.

All I can do is point into the barn.

Everybody cranes round the doorframe to look. The fawn is still curled up where I left her, but Hoopdee is alert on his feet beside her, standing security. When he sees us, he lifts his lip and shows us a tooth or two.

Lady takes this picture in. "Oh for pity's sake, Lyndie! *This* is why you were truant from school on your first day, and nearly gave us all heart failure? To play with a wild animal?"

"I wasn't playing—"

"Now you've got your scent all over that deer. Its mother won't take up with it again."

"Its mother was nowhere," I say. "Besides, I heard that whole smelling-like-a-human thing is a myth."

"Don't you *dare* sass me," Lady snaps. "You have no way to know where its mother is. The laws of nature will decide what's best for that animal. You'll put it right back where you found it."

"My auntie raised up a yearling deer one time," Dawn says. "It was the cutest thing. It followed her all around her yard. But it started eating her cabbages."

"Well, this thing is not going to be eating our cabbages," Lady says. "Or our carrots." She glowers at me. "Child, tell me that is not blood spots I see on your blouse."

"She's hurt," I say. "She's not a thing. Her name is Velvet. I want to help her. There's room in the barn."

"No," Lady says.

"Only till she gets well," Dawn says, all helpfulness.

I scurry into the barn and fall to my knees next to Velvet. "Right," I say. "Until she can run again." I'm hoping Daddy will back me up, but he's got his hands on his hips and an expression that bores through me like a drill. He's having none of me this time.

"Maybe a few months?" My voice goes up high at the end and I recognize that I'm pleading. I pull Velvet into my lap. "So she's well enough to fend for herself."

I can't cry, I *won't* cry. If Lady sees me go weak now, I'll never get to keep my deer.

50

"We can take care of the fawn, if you can't," Dawn pipes up. "Then you can come see her anytime, Lyndie."

Mrs. Spurlock says, "No, we can't, Dawn. We have the boy coming." Mrs. Spurlock gasps. Her eyes widen. "Oh, my word. The *boy*. Social services is bringing him at four o'clock. What time is it?" She shoves the pie plate at Lady. "I brought pie."

Lady takes the plate and shoots me a look that locks me up jaw to knees. "We hardly deserve your delicious shoofly pie, Jessie," she says grimly. "You are *too* kind."

"Oh, Lady," Mrs. Spurlock gushes. "I wish we could stay and help you. You must be . . . But we really have to run." She grabs Dawn by the elbow and pulls away. "If we miss the social services . . ."

They're already halfway through the yard and hustling toward the path. Dawn sends me a wave. "See you tomorrow!" she calls over her shoulder. "You're going to looooove school this year!"

Lady watches them go. "What a crying shame Jessie Spurlock couldn't stay to help me," she says, enunciating every syllable, "get control of my *own granddaughter*."

Daddy lets out an impatient breath. Where he was calm and still, drinking from that whiskey bottle only minutes ago, now he is nervy again, twitching his shoulders under

51

his T-shirt. He says, "Let the little doe heal up, Mama." Daddy's words are full of points and angles. Has Lady noticed how pale he looks?

"Let me get this straight," Lady says. "Your daughter plays truant. Ruins her school clothes . . ." She waves a hand at my crumpled, dusty blazer on the barn floor. "And *humiliates* me in front of Jessie Spurlock. So now—"

"A week or two ought to put her leg right. She's old enough she's probably already weaned," Daddy says sharply.

"Oh for the love of Pete!" Lady cries. "You can't be serious! I am not running a shelter for homeless animals!"

"A pack of coyotes would kill this fawn before the night's out, the condition she's in!" Daddy explodes. "You saying you want to put her out to die, Mama? We can't see our way to give this creature a few nights of peace and safety, before we turn her out?"

Lady goes silent. She watches Daddy.

"I want to help her." My voice trembles. "I will take care of her."

"Quiet, Lyndie!" Daddy turns on me, ferocious. "Get this deer healed up! You have two weeks." He has never used that tone with me in my life.

Velvet's heartbeat quickens under my fingers, matching

my own. I can't speak, so I only nod. Two weeks. Like staying out all night with Daddy after Trilby's funeral, taking care of Velvet feels like exactly the right thing.

"Son," Lady starts, but Daddy cuts her off.

"I expect your grandma has some new rules for you to follow, from here on," Daddy says. Still with that razor edge in his voice. "And rightly so. You broke our trust, Lyndie. You disappointed us all." Daddy's words slice into me.

"She needed help," I mumble.

"Her and the whole world does too," says Daddy. "You'd best take care, what you lend your heart to."

Lyndie's Daily Schedule (courtesy of Lady Hawkins)

5:45 a.m.: Wake up. Get dressed. Brush teeth.

6 a.m.: Put coffeepot on for grown-ups. Eat breakfast.

6:30 a.m.: Feed pets.

7 a.m. **At The Latest***: Leave for school.

2:30-2:45 p.m.: Run home. ("No lollygagging.")

3 p.m. to 4 p.m.: Chores. Clean barn. Pick up bedroom.

4 p.m. to 5 p.m.: Homework. Phone calls for schoolwork only.
Fifteen-minute maximum on phone.

5:30 p.m.: Help get supper and set table.

6:00 p.m.: Eat supper. ("Sit up straight." "Elbows off table.")

6:30 p.m.: Carry dishes in. Dry dishes. Put out trash.
Feed animals.

7-7:30 p.m.: Various chores.**

7:45 p.m.: Tea and cookies with Lady in the parlor.

8 p.m.: Bath. Lay out clean uniform for school. Brush teeth.

8:15 p.m.: Good night to Ma and Daddy. Bed.

Repeat. Repeat. Repeat. Repeat. Repeat.

Notations from Lady:

*Wear the Cinderella watch I put on your nightstand to keep your schedule.

**Various chores schedule is taped to icebox. Monday: Water Boston ferns in parlor. Tuesday: Clean and reset mousetraps under porch, etc.

CHAPTER SIX

This morning, when I wake up, I hear Daddy retching in his room next door. When I knock, he groans and tells me to go on to school.

"Daddy? Are you sick?" I call through the door.

"No!" he yells. "Go on now!"

I dash downstairs and find a bottle of Kaopectate in the kitchen cabinet. Which tastes foul like chalk, but does help upset stomachs, so I run it back upstairs and open Daddy's door a crack and set it inside.

Ma is still in bed. Today is her day off from Miller's. I slide a quick note under her door. "A little deer is in the barn," it says. Maybe enough to tempt her to get up and investigate.

At 6:31 a.m. by my Cinderella watch, I feed Velvet oatmeal and milk. Put Hoopdee's kibble in a bowl next to hers at 6:33. I only have time to give them some good advice for the day—"No romping in the vegetable garden, Hoopdee." "Steer clear of Lady." "Don't annoy Daddy." "If Ma comes out, be sweet."—before I hit the path down to Dawn's house at 6:46.

Dawn is always way early for everything, most especially school. Unlike me, Dawn *loves* school. Every year she runs for class president. Sometimes she wins. Mostly she doesn't. But losing the race never puts a crimp in Dawn's optimism. Dawn always sees the upside in any situation.

I hike my skirt up to crawl over Dawn's fence, craning all around looking for her. I have bucket loads of stuff to tell her—how Velvet already seems to recognize her name, Lady's hideous new schedule, being full-on grounded, and my depressing bedroom. I have even more things *not* to tell her. Much as I love Dawn, I know she couldn't keep a secret if she had it on a leash.

I spot her up ahead, even earlier than usual today, her brushed and shiny bangs bobbing. *The criminal boy* is with her—dropped off yesterday afternoon from social services, I suppose. Dawn has a ball of green yarn in her bag and knitting needles clicking like mad. She is the only person I ever met who can knit while walking. I bet she's starting early on her Holiday Hats for the Homeless.

"Hey!" I call after them, and pick up speed. "Wait up!"

But they're yakking away, so they don't hear me.

I guess he does look a little bit criminal? If criminals are now dressing like they belong in a boy band? He's pretty tall for a seventh grader. He's got a good deal of jiggle around his middle, and gelled-up, spiky black hair. And he's got—seriously—is that a hoop earring in one ear? We do not dress in such costumes around these parts, and we *especially* do not dress in blue-jean jackets with turned up collars at Covenant Academy.

This time the Spurlock family has taken their do-gooding and charity projects one step too far. Knitting hats for the homeless, or whipping up money donations for poor neighbors, or even shoveling out shoofly pies for every church bake sale or friend with the sniffles—I suppose that's harmless. But moving a juvenile delinquent into your *own home* for a whole school year?

Dawn is walking fast. The traffic stops, and the safety monitor waves them across Main Street, onto the median between the busy traffic lanes. I start jogging to try to catch up. Dawn's got a voice that carries. She's talking over her shoulder, fingers busy untangling green yarn.

"After-school clubs," she is saying. "Debate, Chess Kings, Young Rotarians . . ." Dawn already has this kid's entire life in hand, sounds like. Sort of like she straightened my life out, once. She came and sat on the bench where I was reading. And after we got to be friends, she made me pull up my knee socks, and tuck in my shirt, and chew with my mouth closed. I still got in dust-ups and got made fun of, after Dawn took up with me. But not so often.

Dawn swivels around and catches sight of me. "Lyndie!" She waves.

Earring boy nudges Dawn and says something to her. Dawn bursts out laughing. He's been at Spurlocks' one single day, and she's already giggling at him? Holy moly. Dawn, who is practically joke-proof, at least where I am concerned. The space between us suddenly feels as long and curvy as the road from Love's Forge to Cherokee, North Carolina.

Dawn waves her knitting at me. She mouths something—"Later?" "Loser?" I'm not sure.

"Hey!" Somebody bawls in my ear. "Don't you move!" The safety monitor is pointing at her sign. I'm three steps off the curb, walking right into a swiftly flowing river of cars and school buses.

"What color is this, girl?" she vents into my face. "What does this word *say*?"

The sign is red. It says STOP.

"Get back there now." She points at the scrum of kids bunched on the curb behind me. I turn around and shuffle back toward the sidewalk. The light on the median turns green, and Dawn and the boy cross the street, too far away now to hear me even if I yelled.

"Let her walk!" PeeWee Bliss shouts. "She looks like roadkill anyways." His buddies *yuk, yuk, yuk.*

"Oh *good one,* PeeWee," I mutter. PeeWee Bliss is a bucktoothed jackass with porridge for brains, and I'm getting ready to tell him so. But Daddy's face swims up from the back of my brain. *"You disappointed us all."* I snap my mouth shut and ball my fists in my pockets. If Dawn were with me now, she'd know how to handle this.

I move a couple of steps aside to put some air between me and PeeWee.

"Hey, Roadkill." PeeWee Bliss won't quit. "Heard the whole police force was up at your grandma's place Sunday. Were you and your Commie mother building bombs up there? Trying to overthrow America or something?"

Two sophomore boys behind PeeWee, Cecil Fawkes and Tom Hoofnagle, snicker. My head prickles.

PeeWee has hated me with a radiant malice ever since I started at Covenant in third grade. PeeWee's dad got killed fighting in Vietnam when he was only a little baby. His mom has to raise PeeWee and his little sister Darla by herself. PeeWee's mom works full-time managing the K'ream 'n' K'one downtown, plus an extra night shift job doing hotel laundry. PeeWee is the only brown kid in the whole of Covenant Academy, on account of his dad's family is black and his mom is white, which hardly ever happens in Love's Forge. We are not exactly the Rainbow Coalition around here.

PeeWee used to yell at me, that *his* father was the *real* hero who died for his country. And everybody knew my mom was a traitor Communist-loving war protestor peacenik, even though Ma has long since given up protesting against anything. PeeWee said probably my dad was a *coward,* because how else would he have got home in one piece, when all the other veterans in Love's Forge came back in bags or else with body parts missing? Which is not true, I know of several other veterans who are not missing any pieces, at least so far as I can see. For instance, Lewis Bushyhead, who works part-time at the History Museum and also at Hillbilly Hideaway Souvenir Shop in downtown Love's Forge.

Well, by the second time PeeWee yelled this at me when we were third graders, I couldn't stand for him trashtalking my family. We had it out in the playground fair and square, one recess. First, I gave him a solid lecture about our American rights, which say that anybody who wants to can march and protest and make all kinds of hullaballoo for whatever cause they believe in.

Then, I beat him pretty good in front of the whole lower school student body of Covenant Academy. I got sent home early that day, and Ma gave me a serious talk about non-violence. Word got around that my ma was a traitor to America. And worse, that the new kid—me—was ill-mannered and a fighter. A week later, I blurted out in religion class that there was no proof of God being real, any more than there was proof George Washington chopped down a cherry tree. I only meant it as an observation. But I got called an "atheist," and lots worse. After that, it was all over for me at Covenant.

PeeWee was constantly ambushing me, threatening to cut my ear off with round-edge scissors, or gouge out my eye with a sharpened pencil. PeeWee is half as big as a minute, even now, but he has huge emotions, all of which revolve around grudges.

That was when Dawn took up with me. I never could figure out exactly why she picked me to be friends with. At first I was a little suspicious. Then I was grateful.

The thing is, I do feel sorry that PeeWee has no dad. But

no matter what PeeWee says, I know my daddy fought as hard as PeeWee's. And Ma is no traitor.

Now I spin around, ready to give PeeWee a good tongue-lashing.

But when I get a full view of him, he is small and damp-looking, with his shoes all scuffed and the laces tied wrong. I take in the mustard stain on his blazer collar, his scrawny, unwashed neck, and the fight starts to seep out of me. Anybody whose shoes are scuffed like that, wearing a stained blazer on the second day of seventh grade, you have to wonder, is anybody helping him at all, while his mom is working two jobs?

I hitch the mended strap of my book bag up on my shoulder.

Maybe, at least for today, I have no fight with PeeWee.

The monitor flips her sign to green. The kids on my curb buzz forward in a wave of towheads and ski-jump noses.

Across the quad, Covenant Baptist Academy looms up, a brick building that has all the personality of a coma. Covenant is basically a larger version of my grandma Lady, full of lots of rules and schedules. The only enthusiasm you're allowed to show at this school is an enthusiasm for doing exactly what you're told.

At 7:17 by my Cinderella watch, Dawn slides through

the kid-crowd like a butter knife through a tub of Parkay margarine. Dawn evidently has a mission to get earring boy to the front office to check in with mean Miss Smitty and our principal, Pastor Jinks. But I have to check in for my first school day too, so why doesn't she wait for me? Dawn and the boy vanish through the yawning front doors of Covenant Academy.

At 7:20, I see Dawn, down the hall, leave the front office, minus the juvenile delinquent, and wind away through all the kids loitering at their lockers, hurrying so she'll be early to homeroom.

At 7:23, in the front office, Miss Smitty chews me out with barely suppressed enthusiasm for skipping school. Then she huffs off to make copies on the mimeograph machine. There are only two chairs in the office for students who are in some kind of trouble.

I have no choice. I sit down right next to the criminal.

CHAPTER SEVEN

I scooch my chair away a couple of inches and nod at him. Close up, the new kid looks only mildly dangerous. But who can tell what evil lurks in the hearts of boys? Could be, he's hiding a switchblade in all that mess of gelled-up hair. But truly, I'm not so much worried about getting stabbed by the criminal boy as I am about facing Pastor Jinks for skipping the first day of school. I sit there knocking my knees together out of pure nervousness.

The kid takes out a box of jujubes, shakes a handful into his palm, and starts sorting them by color. "Purple," he mutters. "Not a natural food color."

"Eggplant is purple," I say, glancing at the pastor's closed door. "Beets." Worst case scenario, I'm thinking, is the pastor gets under my skin, makes me talk too much, and then calls Ma in for a family conference. No, wait. Worst case is, he calls Lady in. I consider making a run for it.

"Exactly my point," he says. "Those are not even real foods."

I'm exasperated. But I don't need to be rude to a new boy, even if he is a delinquent. I was new once, and I know how that went. "Sorry?"

"So, what are you in here for?" he says.

"I missed school yesterday."

"No kidding. You skipped. That shoofly pie? It was supposed to be my welcome pie. We had canned pears for dessert last night. Instead of pie."

"Cry me a river," I say.

"I sure hope you enjoyed it. That delicious welcome treat didn't belong anywhere near your pie-hole."

"If you are so omni-knowing, you should also know I *didn't get to eat* any pie."

"Okay, now you have my sympathy." He offers me a palmful of purple jujubes. "You must be dangerously sugar-depleted. Breakfast?"

I wave my hand at his candy. "Your dentist must love you."

"Candy for breakfast, candy for lunch, then a sensible dinner," he says. "It's a foolproof way to shed pounds and lose inches." He shakes out another handful. "Don't tell Dawn, though."

I glance at the pastor's door again, and then at Miss Smitty, busy at the mimeograph machine. I could just slip out and go to homeroom, but since I wasn't here yesterday, I have no idea what homeroom I'm supposed to be in.

"Dawn doesn't approve of my diet regimen," he says through a gummy mouthful of candy.

Irritation digs into my ribs. I turn and look at him full-on. "How would you know if Dawn does or does not approve of your candy habit? You met her like thirteen hours ago."

"True," he says. "But it was love at first sight. On Dawn's part."

I snort. Because this is purely ridiculous. Nobody is going to be crushing on this pudgy boy with his spiky hairdo. Even so, this kid has spent more time with Dawn in thirteen hours than I have in thirteen days. I miss Dawn something fierce.

"Unfortunately, I don't think Dawn will have much time to romance me," he adds. "She's pretty busy planning her campaign for seventh-grade president, come November. She's already secured my vote."

I stare at him, flummoxed. Then I do bust out laughing—I can't help it. He's got Dawn totally pegged. "Not to mention, busy feeding the hungry and homeless."

"Mmm-hmm. That too." He chews thoughtfully. "Lucky for me."

First bell rings, and out in the hall, there's the last scuffle of kids running for homeroom. Then the hall goes dead quiet. The clock above Miss Smitty's mimeograph machine goes *tick, tick, tick* in time with my Cinderella watch, each *tick* bringing me closer to my rendezvous with Pastor Jinks.

"Nice watch," he says. "For a four-year-old."

"Nice hair," I retort. "If you want to fit in around here, you might start with a new haircut. The one you've got does not really flatter you."

"Don't take this wrong." He crumples the empty box of jujubes and lobs it into Miss Smitty's wastebasket in a perfect, overhand arc. "But I don't think you should be giving anybody advice about *fitting in*."

"Oh, that stings."

"Wow. Dawn didn't warn me you were so crusty, Lyndie Hawkins. What I heard was, Lyndie is the *best*. She has the *coolest* mom and the *coolest* dad. Lives with the *sweetest* grandparents. Owns one *adorable* hound dog, and now, the *most darling* baby deer with a broken leg, named Violet."

"The deer's name is Velvet. And her leg is not broken." I'm secretly pleased to find out Dawn and this kid have been talking about me so much. It does sound exactly like what Dawn would say. She's always looking on the bright side. "What a *buttinski* you are," I add.

"Is that word on the final exam?"

I blink at him.

"Okay, okay," he says. "Could I at least get a synonym? I really need to hit the vocabulary hard this year."

I keep my face blank, but I'm smiling a little inside. "I don't think *buttinski* is going to be on our exam," I tell him. "*Intrusive* might be, though."

Mean Miss Smitty marches over holding a stack of math tests, reeking of mimeograph ink. She's glaring at me. Obviously, I'm going to have to really buckle down if I want Miss Smitty to forgive my truancy.

"Lyndon. The pastor will see you. He's on the phone now *with your grandmother*." She pauses to let the horror of this sink in. "You can go in when he's finished. D.B., we need to get you a Covenant Academy uniform. We have strict regulations. About hair too." She scrutinizes D.B. with no evidence of any goodwill. "The earring will have to go," she says. "You might as well take it off now. And denim is a forbidden fabric." She stalks off and rummages around in her desk.

"A *forbidden fabric*." D.B. chortles. "I like the whole notion of that." He tosses a red jujube into the air and catches it in his mouth.

"So what's *D.B.* stand for?"

"Damned Brilliant." He fiddles with his earring, takes it off, drops it in his jacket pocket.

"Not much evidence of that yet," I say. "More like, Dingle Berry?"

"Very funny."

"What's it stand for, then?"

"Disturbed Boy."

"Oh. Well, I was thinking, you seem sort of well adjusted. Considering."

"It's a ruse," he says, shrugging. He peels off his blue-jean jacket and folds it neatly over the back of his chair. He's wearing a T-shirt printed with the words: *Frankie Says Relax*.

D.B. darts a glance around the office and lowers his voice. "So, what do I need to know about Covenant Academy? Other than which fabrics are forbidden."

"What, Dawn didn't fill you in?"

"Dawn loves school. I need the quick and dirty."

"Oh, man," I say. "Where do I start? Covenant is not a good place to be, but probably better than juvenile reform school. Hopefully, a pair of khaki trousers and a blue blazer with the Covenant insignia will give you secret camouflage. Nobody will ever guess the truth, that you're a juvenile delinquent."

He barks out a laugh. "I've been here thirteen hours, as

you pointed out, and I already totally see that everybody knows *everything* about everybody around here. So, I've got to ace all my exams this year. But, let's say I happen to slip up—in some non-exam-related way." He jabs his thumb at the pastor's closed door. "What kind of whipping do I get from the pastor?"

"Pastor Jinks doesn't whip," I say. "He's not like that. He stopped the teachers paddling us when he came last year. They're not allowed to hit us anymore."

He looks truly surprised at this. "No lie?"

"For real. And he makes you contemplate yourself. Which is worse than a paddling. He gets you to tell stuff you don't want to tell."

D.B.'s face has gone a shade pink. He jumps up and shakes all over like a wet dog. "I'm already sick of sitting in a chair and it's only—" He points to my watch. "What does Cinderella say?"

"Seven forty-five. So, where you came from, do they hit you?"

He hops from foot to foot.

Miss Smitty, at her desk, is noisily shuffling what looks like pages and pages of uniform regulations. She looks up, scowls at D.B., and points to his chair. He plops back down with a sigh.

"Where were you at?" I say.

He makes a grim face. "Pure Visions Reform Academy. Otherwise known as the Worst. Place. On. Earth."

I whisper, "Did you really commit a crime?"

He shrugs. "That's what they say."

"What do *they say* you did?"

He raises his eyes to meet mine. I notice he's got one green eye and one brown one, which is sort of like looking at two different people at once. "Now who's the buttinski?"

"You may as well tell me. Dawn surely will."

He looks ready to say something snarky. But he stops and his brow furrows. He drops his eyes.

"But okay. You don't have to tell me, if you don't want to."

He sits there staring at his high-tops, and his face goes from shiny to dull. Finally, he says, "It was a stupid accident." He sounds like the words are stuck somewhere between his heart and his mouth.

"Oh." I play with the pleats in my plaid skirt, not sure what to say.

After a minute, he braces his shoulders and says: "I promised myself, before I left Pure Visions. If anybody asked what I did, I would tell the truth."

"That's a little weird. But okay."

"If I tell the truth, I don't have to go back."

I don't tell him I kind of doubt that's how it works.

His fists are balled on his knees. He says, "I set our house on fire."

"Holy cow," I breathe.

"It got out of control," he says.

I don't know what I'd guessed he'd gotten in trouble for. Maybe getting in fights or throwing rocks through windows or stealing Baby Ruth bars from Woolworth's. But burning down your own house? How would you even do that?

I ask carefully, "Was anybody hurt in the fire? Where were your parents?"

"Foster parents." He exhales, blinking. "My foster dad died." When he glances up from his high-tops, he must see the shock in my face. "No, no, he didn't die from the fire—the fire only burnt the top story. He died last week, they told me. Pure Visions wouldn't even let me go to his funeral! Because he wasn't a blood relation. They said it was *against policy.*"

"That's terrible." Something goes very soft in me. "Wow. I'm—that's terrible." It would be good for the pastor to open his door and wave me inside now, away from this fascinating and dreadful conversation. "Hey," I say. "Maybe the Spurlocks can keep you?"

"Nah," he says. "They can't. Trial Release is only for one school year."

"But if it's a trial, and you do okay, shouldn't you go free? Isn't that the whole point of having a *trial*?"

"If I get perfect grades and get in no trouble, the best I can hope is—"

But Miss Smitty puts down the phone at her desk, and she is on us again, all business. "D.B., you're with me. Lyndon Hawkins." She points at the door. "The pastor is ready for you."

I stand, brushing my skirt flat and pulling down my sweater. D.B. looks very glum. Did I ask too many personal questions?

I give him a half smile. D.B. looks away. *"Take care, what you lend your heart to,"* I hear Daddy's voice in my head. I straighten my back, inhale, and go in to see Pastor Jinks.

CHAPTER EIGHT

Second-period bell rings as I'm coming out of the pastor's office. Miss Smitty thrusts my class schedule into my hand—another schedule!—and hustles me off in the direction of Advanced English with Mrs. Flannigan on the second floor.

I dash upstairs trying to outrun one extra worry: What I told the pastor and definitely should not have. Pastor Jinks has a sixth sense about kid trouble. He can dig around inside your partway lies and non-answers until he finds something real underneath.

"Let's meet tomorrow with your grandmother and your father—if he's available," the pastor suggested. "I met your grandma and mother last year. Your daddy is still a mystery."

In classroom 217, fifteen kids are on their feet, joking and horsing around, but no teacher.

Dawn's up in the front row, but Hillary Baggett is already in the desk next to her, yakking her ear off. I suppose they're good buddies now, since they do dancing class on Friday nights. Looks like I missed a lot while I was packing boxes this summer. Much as I want to talk to Dawn, I can't deal with Hillary. So I grab a desk toward the back of the room, scanning to see who I know.

Horace Wise is in here. No surprise. He's a brain. Sara Jane Hart, already looking peevish about being separated from Hillary by two whole desks. A trio of obnoxious boys: Jarrod Pierce. Frank Stoppard. PeeWee Bliss—wait, what? PeeWee Bliss? In Advanced English? How is that possible?

Mrs. Flannigan strides through the door with an armful of worksheets, D.B. trailing behind her. Miss Smitty has worked her magic: He's got on a school uniform, and his hair is cut short. Not one single element of that uniform fits right—it bags where it should hug and hugs where it should bag. Definitely, this uniform is not going to work as camouflage.

The kids in the room quiet down, one by one, to check out D.B. We don't ever get new kids here. Does anybody besides me and Dawn know he's a criminal? An arsonist?

"Class, take your seats." Mrs. Flannigan points. "D.B.,

take that desk right there." D.B. trundles over to a desk in the third row and plops down.

"Where is Lyndon Hawkins?" Mrs. Flannigan scans the room. Reluctantly, I raise my hand. "I'm glad you could join us today." She gives me a close look. "See me after class, and I'll catch you up on our rules and procedures."

Yay.

"Horace." She shoves her bundle of paper at Horace Wise. "Pass these out please? We're going to try something a bit different this year. Instead of writing about *ourselves,* we're going to begin with studying *one another's* lives. We're going to investigate them through a narrative lens."

Papers stop rustling and everybody looks up. This *is* different from what we usually do in English. Year after year, we spend the first week writing about what we did on our summer vacation, or what we love most about our moms. And after that, every second of classroom time is devoted to diagramming sentences, taking spelling tests, and identifying main ideas, with no relief in sight. Could this be the meaning of *Advanced*?

"What do I mean by *narrative*?" Mrs. Flannigan asks.

I believe she means each person's life, if you know enough about it, can be made into a story with a beginning, a middle, and an end. It can have heroes and villains, adventure and sorrow, unexpected twists, and happy or sad endings. I know this from reading about Abe Lincoln. And also about Robert Smalls, who was enslaved and then stole a boat and joined the Union Army and then later became a member of Congress! They were real people with some pretty thrilling narratives. But I'm not about to volunteer any of that. I've been laughed at in too many classrooms over my time at Covenant to ever say out loud what I think, or worse, disagree with. Nobody likes a know-it-all, which I can sort of be.

"*Narrative* means 'story,'" says Hillary Baggett. Hillary is a know-it-*sometimes* who is allowed to act smart (and wear glitter eye shadow, I guess) because she is pretty and her family donated enough money to Covenant. The new lower-school building is Baggett Hall.

"Thank you, Hillary. A story, where there is a connection between events. For your first project, you will identify the narrative elements in your team's life stories: the major conflicts, the character traits, even perhaps the theme of each person's life."

Wow. I sense the mysterious hand of Pastor Jinks here. The pastor started to talk about the "spirit of inquiry" as soon as he got to Covenant last year.

Dawn sits up straighter and looks over her shoulder, catching my eye. I throw her a hopeful smile.

"You're going to begin your investigation working in teams of four. This is a two-week project. Week one, we will spend exploring one another's stories. Week two will be devoted to oral presentations. There will be research.

"Now count off. Horace, you can begin."

"One," says Horace Wise. "Two," says Jarrod Pierce, behind him. "Three," says PeeWee Bliss on the other side of the room.

"Two," I say when it's my turn.

Dawn jumps to her feet. "Who's a three?"

"That would be me!" D.B. goes over and knocks fists with Dawn.

"Two?" I put my hand tentatively in the air.

Hillary Baggett groans. "Oh. God. *No way*. I'm a two."

"I'm a three," Sara Jane Hart says miserably, making puppy eyes at Hillary.

"Everybody has a story to tell, and unless you ask, you never hear it," Mrs. Flannigan says. "Today, you will interview one another and write preliminary notes on your icebreaker sheets."

Frankly, I would need a jackhammer to *break the ice* with Hillary Baggett.

"This is not happening," Hillary says to Sara Jane. She flounces over to Mrs. Flannigan's desk. Hillary's voice rises in an agonized whine above the shuffle of kids and moving desks. Mrs. Flannigan says something. Hillary counters. Mrs. Flannigan parries. Hillary wheedles.

"Oh, for goodness' sake, Hillary!" Mrs. Flannigan throws her hands up. "This is your only Get Out of Jail Free Card this year. Don't even bother to *ask* me for another favor."

Mrs. Flannigan calls, "Lyndie Hawkins, Sara Jane Hart, switch teams. Lyndie is now a three. Sara Jane is a two."

I glance over at Dawn. PeeWee is standing next to her with his hands shoved in his pockets, glaring at the ceiling.

One hand giveth, the other taketh away, as we've heard repeatedly in morning chapel. Now I've got Dawn on my team, and the new kid, D.B., which is okay. But PeeWee?

"Lyndon, get up and go to your team, please," Mrs. Flannigan says.

I gather up my English book and binder and do as I'm told. Horace hands me a ditto worksheet on my way by.

"Greetings, Planet of the Threes," I say, ignoring Pee-Wee's foul looks. "Take me to your leader."

Dawn is busy pushing desks together. "Hey, Lyndie!" she says. "Cool we're on the same team." D.B. helps her arrange desks.

"Maybe we should give ourselves a fashionable name," I say brightly. "Teams always have names. It builds cohesion."

"That's an idea," Dawn says.

"Co-he-shun," PeeWee mutters. "Big words, small minds."

I grab the only desk that is not next to PeeWee, but that means I'm facing him directly. The look on his face is sort of murderous.

"Thick as Threes?" I offer. "Three's a Crowd?"

Nobody laughs. Dawn says, "PeeWee, this is D.B. He's new."

PeeWee barely acknowledges D.B. We all get busy reading the instructions on our worksheets.

"This is going to be fun." Dawn beams around. "Let's pair up to do the questionnaires, it's more efficient." I widen my eyes at her and shake my head in PeeWee's direction. PeeWee will stab out my eyeballs before he'll work with me one-on-one. Dawn knows. "You and D.B. be partners," she directs. "D.B. and I already had tons of time to find out about each other."

D.B. sits reading, twirling his pencil.

"Hey." I nudge him. "Here's your chance to start getting good grades. I can help with that."

He grunts, not in an unfriendly way. I guess he's embarrassed for telling me too much about himself in the front office earlier. I determine not to mention fires, or dead foster fathers, or juvenile detention centers, no matter what.

I scan down the worksheet. "Let's get started," I say. "Full name?"

"*D* for *Definitely*. *B* for *Beefcake*."

I grin. "Nice haircut, by the way. Guess you took my advice."

"Miss Smitty about took off my right ear," he says. "Which would be a shame, since my right ear is my best feature."

"It sure is purdy," I drawl. "Like a little pink seashell."

"I don't even know why I'm in Advanced English," he says. "I've hardly ever read a book from page one to the end."

"Maybe you test well. Okay, let's take turns asking questions. What's the *D.B.* really stand for?"

D.B. purses up his lips. Hesitates. "Dee-Ell Baily. But it's spelled *D-A-L-Z-E-L-L*."

"What kind of name is that?"

"A kind of name that wins you no friends. Especially not in a juvenile correction facility."

"Come on."

"Hold up. Is that question on the worksheet?"

"Yes it is, right here. It says, *Is it a family name? Why did your parents choose it?*"

"It's a Scottish name. My turn."

"Lyndon Baines Hawkins." I save him the trouble of

asking. "Lyndie, for short. Named after President Lyndon Baines Johnson."

D.B. raises an eyebrow.

"Doesn't matter. Next."

"Birthday?"

"September twenty-eighth." It's a couple of weeks away, but I haven't even thought about my birthday. Neither has anybody else, seems like.

"What's your family's origin?" I ask, sensing this question is moving into perilous territory.

"My foster family or birth family?"

"Wait. You have both?"

"You can't *not* have a birth family!" he says. "It's totally my turn, anyway. Question: How many donuts can you eat in one sitting?"

I bug my eyes at him. "That is definitely *not* on the worksheet. And, you didn't tell me where Dee-Ell comes from."

"If you could be any flavor of ice cream, what would you be? Explain in detail."

"Again, not on the worksheet. Plus. I don't *want* to be ice cream. Too drippy, plus you get eaten alive."

"Rocky road," D.B. pretends to write. "Nuts on the inside."

"You're a riot. What did you like most about your first home?" I read off the paper.

Then I wish I could suck the words back down my throat. I duck my head. You can't ask this question to a foster care kid who lives in a juvenile correction facility! I scan down the worksheet looking for a safer question. I already know the answers to some of these, even though I probably shouldn't.

I raise my eyes from the worksheet in confusion. How much are we supposed to know about other people's private business?

"What did I like about my first home?" D.B. asks. "First one I can remember, anyway. I went to stay at my nana's house for the summer, in Florida. Nana made me sugar and butter sandwiches. Big heaps of them. She let me eat as many as I wanted."

"Sugar and butter sandwiches—are you joking?"

"On Wonder Bread. I never tasted anything so delicious before that." He smiles.

"When was that? How old were you?"

"I was . . . I think . . . six?" D.B.'s smile wavers.

"Five minutes," Mrs. Flannigan calls. "Wrap it up."

"My turn," D.B. says. But his whole mood has changed. "What is your family origin?" he asks woodenly.

"English. Hawkinses come from colonists who lived in the Province of North Carolina," I say. I've been told this so many times. "They were among the first Americans."

He stops writing and tosses down his pencil, rolling his eyes. "Oh! Okay. So, when your ancestors arrived, the whole place was empty? Nobody living here at all, is that right?" He sounds really irritated.

I feel my face flushing. "I didn't mean—"

"Just empty space, as far as the eye could see. . . ."

"Hey, I happen to know native people were here. I know lots about it. I didn't mean it that way."

"Hello, they were here for like *fifty thousand years* before a single Hawkins ever set foot." D.B. seems weirdly, unpredictably passionate on this subject.

Lady and Grandpa Tad always talk about our families being the first to live here. And I never thought about it before, how they happily skip over fifty thousand years, like it's nothing.

The only person in Love's Forge who ever talks about what went on with native people in Tennessee is Mrs. Dooley at the library. She's the one who showed me *The Cherokee Indian Nation: A Troubled History,* and didn't even blink when I checked out the book three times. I read this book aloud to Ma and Daddy when we took our road trip to Alabama to visit Granny and Auntie Pearl two years ago.

"They were among the first *white* settlers," I correct myself. Not so special.

"What about your mother's side?"

"What about it?" I glance at PeeWee. Let's not get him started on my mother.

"Her maternal parent . . ." D.B. pretends to write. "Was born . . . under a cabbage leaf. In Mr. McGregor's garden."

"Oh, doesn't she wish," Hillary Baggett says loudly. "It's not that fascinating. Her mama is nothing but hippie Alabama trash. Her mom's name is *Rainbow*. Pathetic."

Oh. She did not say that!

"Pathetic," Sara Jane echoes like a demented parrot.

"Boo-hoo, Lonely Little Lyndie," Hillary singsongs.

PeeWee's head jolts up like a hound dog scenting a possum. Dawn stops her monologue and tries to catch my eye.

"Hippie *Commie* Alabama Trash!" PeeWee crows.

Every student within hearing range turns to watch us with bottomless interest.

I grit my teeth. I'm not going to cat-fight with Hillary or fistfight with PeeWee on only my first day of school, no matter how much they needle me. I've already got Lady—and possibly Daddy, who has been in a bad mood getting worse by the day—coming in for a conference tomorrow.

I snatch up D.B.'s pencil and hunker over our papers, stopping my ears to the tittering. They don't know the first *thing* about me or my family.

"Look." I turn D.B.'s worksheet over. I trace a rough

map of Tennessee, North Carolina, and Alabama. "*H* is for *Hawkins,* my daddy's people. They settled in Greene County in 1780." I put an *H* and a star around the area where Greeneville would be, for the Hawkins Homestead. "The old log house my great-granddaddy built is still there, after all this time. Grandpa Tad's auntie, Miss Francine, she went all around Tennessee and tried to convince plantation owners to let the people they enslaved buy their freedom, but she was only part successful."

D.B. nods. "That's cool."

"*M* is for *McKenzie,* my mama's people. Her grandparents moved from Tuscaloosa, Alabama, with all their things in a mule cart, and came to make a new home in Love's Forge, here. Now there's only two McKenzies left, my granny and my auntie Pearl. They live in Tuscaloosa."

"And *B* is for *brat,* which is what came along after Hawkins met McKenzie," pipes up Hillary behind me.

Titter, titter, titter goes our audience.

I add stars for Tuscaloosa and Love's Forge, my tongue between my teeth. If I could bash up Hillary Baggett, it would put a spring in my step for a week. Why does she have to be so nasty about my family? She doesn't hardly know us except from gossip.

"The McKenzies were running from trouble they got

into from faith-healing sick people in Tuscaloosa," I explain in a low voice to keep the others from hearing.

"It sounds like your family is—complicated," D.B. says. "Welcome to my world."

"Hey guys," Dawn says. "Two minutes?"

Tick, tick, tick goes my Cinderella watch, fastened to my wrist like a handcuff.

D.B. looks at me, and our eyes meet. He sits a little taller. "Thanks for showing me this, Lyndie. The Hawkinses and McKenzies. It was really interesting." His voice carries over Hillary and Sara Jane and PeeWee.

And it *is* interesting. At least to me. Everything about the Hawkinses and McKenzies. And then all those years later, Ma walking out of her classes to go march with so many other college students to end the Vietnam War—at the same time Daddy was fighting over there. But the kids at school don't care or even have any curiosity about any of it. Even Dawn only half listens, mostly because she's polite. "Thanks for listening, D.B."

"*C* is for *Commie!*" PeeWee says to Sara Jane, who bursts out laughing.

"*D* is for *Dweeb!*" she chimes in, ridiculously.

Hillary piles it on now. "*Dweeb* is what the *Commie brat* grew up into."

87

"Oh man," I say under my breath. "Oh man. Oh man."

D.B. looks up from my map and stares at Sara Jane and Hillary.

Hillary fastens her glittery gaze on D.B. "Now you know the ABCs of *Lyndon's* people, new boy."

CHAPTER NINE

To keep to Lady's schedule, I jog from my last class, Algebra I, straight to my locker, shove all my books into my book bag and throw the strap over my shoulder, then sprint down the hall with the books bouncing on my hip and out the front door of Covenant.

School lets out at 2:30, and Lady's schedule puts me home at 2:45. I don't have time to find Dawn—her last class is Advanced Algebra II, all the way on a whole other floor.

From Covenant, I have to run flat-out uphill home. Running toward Velvet and Hoopdee and Ma and Daddy makes my feet fly. The happiness spreads up from my feet to my knees and my pumping arms, and into my lungs filling up with clean bright air. I am hoping Ma's headache got better today. I am hoping I can get her to come down and take a look at Lady's garden. That we will decide what weird non-edible root vegetables to plant, like we used to do, until we can get home to our real garden.

The Blue Bullet is in the drive. But Lady's Cadillac is not, thank goodness. Hoopdee woofs from the barn, hearing my running footsteps. When I yank open the heavy door with a squeal of hinges, the barn is cool, sweet smelling, and shadowed. Hoopdee has dragged the blankets I put down all the way over to a safe hidden spot behind Grandpa Tad's machines and scavenged junk, making a cozy home for him and Velvet. He bounds to his feet when he sees me, panting with pride.

I have a full hour for pet-related chores, long as I pick up my room before four o'clock. I fill the hubcap with water and let Velvet and Hoopdee take turns slurping. Velvet makes the cutest noises when she drinks, little snuffly cries of joy. "Did Ma come see you today? Don't worry," I tell her. "Hoopdee and I will take care of you. You will be fine now. We will love you."

She brushes my cheek and my ear and my forehead with her nose. I'm about to put Hoopdee's collar on her, when I realize: She doesn't need a collar any more than I need a Cinderella watch. "Be free!" I tell her. "Live by your own rules!" Her leg is better—not oozing, but scabbing over.

Velvet follows me out of the barn quiet as you please, only limping a little, nibbling my elbow. Hoopdee runs ahead, and we tramp down the path into the woods.

Velvet sniffs at branches, ears perking and twitching. She raises her nose in the air. Sometimes she stops dead still, listening hard for something, a sound that doesn't quite come. Hoopdee romps off scattering sprays of orange leaves, but I stand waiting. Velvet listens. I listen. There's nothing but whispery rustling. No gentle squeaking call from her mother. She drops her head.

At 3:30 on the nose I finish cleaning the barn. The whole world feels still, and the sun is heavy on the Smoky Mountains. Today is okay. Dawn's house is down the hill. She is in my Advanced English class. Also, there's a new Civics and History teacher, Mr. Handy.

The whole point of learning about history, Mr. Handy told us in class, is you figure out that knowledge is changeable. New people come along and retell the story. Every year we are here on Earth, we make little nudges and revisions to what we think about where we came from and what we have done. What we fought for, and why, and whether it was the right thing to do.

D.B. is in Mr. Handy's Civics and History class, and he made me laugh out loud at least six times during our first lesson on Being an American. Hillary and PeeWee and Sara Jane are not in that class, so I can relax.

Through the open barn door, the breeze is soft, rustling through the trees in a way that reminds me of our own cottage at home.

Then, all out of nowhere comes: *Bang! Bang, bang!*

Hoopdee and Velvet and I jump three feet. I sprint from the barn, slamming the door shut. Behind the farmhouse, a flock of crows scatters up in a sudden curtain of fearsome flapping, wheeling in the sky.

I know what that sound is.

Bang! Bang! Bang! Someone shoots a second round. It's too close to be hunters in the woods, and besides, you're not allowed to use guns to hunt deer until October, every kid in Tennessee knows that.

Which can only mean . . .

For a second I stand there trembling. Where is the shooting coming from?

I run on jelly legs. Round back of the farmhouse, there's Daddy on the porch. He reloads a black pistol. Takes aim. He holds his arm out and squints down the barrel. But his arm wobbles. And he's swaying.

Bang! Bang, bang!

Woodchips fly when the bullets hit the big old apple tree.

A crow, a black clump of ruffled feathers, lies dead in the grass.

Daddy's expression is grim and ugly. Where on earth did he get a *gun*?

Bang. Daddy's arm jerks. He misses hitting anything this time and stumbles backward.

I stand glued in place, palms pressed to my ears. Gunshots so close are really loud. I never heard a gun for real before, because about the only thing Ma is still passionate about is: NO WEAPONS IN THE HOUSE.

On the table next to him, in plain sight, is the whiskey bottle I found in his glove box.

It's empty.

Daddy catches sight of me. His stare has no feeling in it, like he's trying to make sense of me. Not disappointed. Not loving or teasing. It's like he's looking down into a hole where his daughter used to be.

The screen door slams behind Daddy. Ma comes tearing out in her bathrobe, eyes flitting across the yard. Daddy lowers his pistol. She knocks the table over when she runs by, and the empty whiskey bottle rolls on the porch floor. Ma spots me and practically throws herself down the steps. Running to me, her arms open.

She scoops me up and holds me like she can't get close enough.

Her hands move over my shoulders, my head and arms. "Baby, you're not hurt?"

The quaver in Ma's voice makes my knees start to shake. My body is not hurt. Daddy is shooting a gun at nothing and the whiskey bottle is empty.

Ma spins back to Daddy. The black gun hangs shivering in his hand.

"Tyrus!" she shouts.

Daddy jumps.

Ma's arms tighten around me. "Put it down! How could you?" Her words are brittle and explosive. "How could you?" she shrieks again. "You promised."

You promised. I think of that morning after the ice storm, after their big fight, when he came down smelling of Aqua Velva, and spent all day that day and many more days after looking for a job. But he hasn't gone out looking since we sold our house and moved in here with Lady and Grandpa Tad.

I watch Ma's face, the fury and disappointment in it.

Daddy looks out over the mountains, his shoulders drooping under his blue chambray shirt.

"Get out!" Ma shouts at him now. Bitterness and betrayal ring all through those two words.

I peer round her shoulder. Daddy raises the gun and

opens the chamber. Shells spill on the porch floor with a sound of rain falling on a tin roof. He does not put the gun down. He shoves the black gun into his belt.

Ma kneels in the grass and makes me kneel down too. She looks into my eyes. "I need you to stay here until I come get you, okay?"

"Ma, what's happening?" I whisper.

She leans her head on my chest. "Stay here, Lyndie?" She breathes a raggedy breath. "Everything will be fine. Please. Don't come into the house until I tell you, okay?"

"All right, Ma. I won't. I promise."

A pigeon rises from behind a stand of bushes with a clumsy whipsaw of wings. Daddy falls back hard at the noise, his face going gray.

He came back different, I hear Lady say in my head. After Trilby's funeral, he came back even more different. No more joking, no more fibbing to Lady. No more shaking pinkies with me. No more saying, *I need Lyndie to help me . . .* Where has he gone, that Daddy who was my best friend?

CHAPTER TEN

Daddy flees, round the side of the farmhouse.

I wait for half an hour by my Cinderella watch. My eyes never leave the screen door. Any moment I expect Ma to come get me, but she doesn't come. After fifteen minutes, I hear the Blue Bullet start up on the other side of the house. The engine roars, and the car churns out of the driveway, with the sound of spinning gravel at the gate. I hold my breath and pin myself to the ground, digging my fingernails into my palms to keep myself rooted.

Daddy is *getting out*.

After five minutes more, Lady's Cadillac purrs up the ridge road and turns in.

Screen door whines open. Screen door slams. After two minutes more, there's a murmur of talking. More minutes *tick, tick, tick*.

At four o'clock on the dot, Lady comes out the back door and finds me hunched in the grass, quivering like a scared rabbit.

My grandmother hustles around the parlor plumping up the brocade pillows on the antique chairs, switching on the lamps one by one. Daddy has been gone four and a half hours. It's a quarter to eight. Right on schedule, it's time for "tea and cookies."

Coming alive in the lamplight, the oil paint portraits of all our rich, thin-lipped ancestors from the beginning of time glower down at me. They look like people who have a home, who have always had a home. And who will never, ever leave it.

I settle gingerly on the edge of one of the musty silk couches, so I won't mess Lady's perfectly positioned pillows. Grandpa Tad is working late at the law office, and Ma has retreated up into her room. But like every other night, Lady is cool as the other side of a pillow. Our lonely supper, me and Lady, was leftover pot roast from last night. Which is now balled up in my stomach like I swallowed wet rags.

My after-supper cookie sits uneaten on the china plate. Lady sits opposite me and bends over her silver tea tray. Steam from the pot rises and fills the air with Earl Grey.

"Pastor Jinks called today," she says. "He wants to meet with us tomorrow morning. I suppose you know that." She swipes a stray white hair back into her up-do. Her face seems to have grown some extra frowns and wrinkles since this morning. "About your truancy, I imagine."

"I don't know," I say miserably. "I guess so. Is Ma coming?"

"She has to work an early shift at Miller's tomorrow."

"He said he wanted to meet Daddy."

"Well," Lady says. "We'll see. Did you water these ferns? They look parched." Lady sits back with her cup, fingering one of the giant Boston ferns next to her chair.

"Yes, Lady."

"Did you check the mousetraps?"

I didn't check the mousetraps. After seeing the body of that poor innocent crow in the yard, I had no desire whatsoever to deal with more dead animals.

"They'll start to smell if you don't clean them out," she says. "We can't have things rotting under the house."

"Lady, can I go see Hoopdee and Velvet?"

The parlor clock ticks, out of synch with my Cinderella watch. Lady has said not one word about Daddy, but she keeps looking out the parlor window, jumping at every creak in the floorboards.

"It's late. You should be getting to bed."

"I'll be quick."

"You don't need to be getting attached to that doe. She'll be gone in a few days, and I won't have you moping."

"Please?"

"You want to be sweet and care for something, there's four people in this household could use your love."

Three people.

"I want you to stick to your schedule, Lyndie. It will help you develop personal discipline. My mama had me keep a schedule when I was your age, and it did wonders for my character." She takes another sip of tea.

Hearing her say those words, "did wonders for my character," makes my legs and arms feel like they are filled with buckshot.

Outside our parlor window, the wind picks up and thunder grumbles. It's pitch-dark, so all I can see is my own wretched reflection, perched on the edge of the silk settee in the lamplight. Why doesn't Daddy come back?

"Can I take Ma up a piece of pie, then?"

"There's no pie."

"How is there no pie?"

"I tossed it out."

"But that's wasteful!"

"Those nosy Spurlocks with their do-gooding charity projects! Interfering where they ought to leave well enough alone. As if they could do all God's work single-handedly."

"Mrs. Spurlock was only being nice. That's how they are. And Dawn would have given that pie to some homeless person, if we weren't going to eat it."

I don't know why I feel like I could break down howling over a two-day-old shoofly pie, but I do.

"Oh, they are very *nice,* Herk and Jessie Spurlock," Lady says. "And Dawn has certainly been more than nice to *you*. But charity begins at home." Lady closes her eyes and leans back into the brocade pillows.

Dawn was nice to me. She followed me around in third grade, talking and pestering when I was new to Covenant, always taking my side. She stepped in between me and PeeWee. Took up for me with Hillary Baggett. Now a horrible idea starts to percolate.

What if Dawn always felt sorry for me, and no more? Like I was charity? That day she came and sat next to me at recess, I had my nose in a book. The other kids were ignoring me. Was that why she was kind to me? Looking out for Lonely Little Lyndie?

"Now," Lady says. "Go right on up to see your mama. Then to bed."

There are books, books, books everywhere around Ma's single bed, and stacks of magazines, like she has trapped herself inside a castle made of words.

She pulls me close, puts her chin on the top of my head. "Talk to me, baby girl."

"Where's Daddy gone?"

"Oh honey. I suppose"—there's a tremble in her voice—"your dad will be back, eventually."

And if he does come back, will he start talking to Ma again? In full sentences with subjects, verbs, and predicates? Will Ma stop staying in bed reading book after book, and go back to being the person I can count on? Or will Daddy come back different again?

I want to ask her how come Daddy has that gun. And what it means that Daddy is secret-drinking whiskey. But I can't.

"Does Lady . . . know?"

"Not yet," Ma says.

"Please, please, Ma. Please don't tell her."

Ma's arms pull me closer. "Maybe you're right. That wouldn't solve anything."

Lady would clamp down on all of us with more rules and schedules and groundings and nagging.

I curl up and put my head in her lap. Ma unbraids my hair, hands warm and soft.

"Ma?"

"Yes, Lyndie."

"Would you tell about the first time you and Daddy met?"

"Oh, surely, not tonight. I would like to take you to see Mama and your auntie Pearl," she says. "In Tuscaloosa. Stay for a while."

We haven't seen Granny and Auntie Pearl since two Easters ago when we went to visit. Granny left the commune about ten years ago, and now she and Auntie Pearl live in a small, hot, concrete house in Tuscaloosa. But Ma must wish, sometimes, to hear her mama's voice or feel her hand playing with her hair.

"I can't leave school now," I say. "Not after already missing a day."

"All right. Maybe someday." She sounds disappointed.

"Tell me," I insist. "Start with the part where you challenge Daddy and his buddies to a game of pool. How did you know?"

Her hands stop braiding.

"How did I know what?"

"The guys at the bar. When you first met Daddy. How did you know they were soldiers?"

"You could see they were soldiers," she says slowly. "They seemed older than the college boys. They wore their feelings all over their faces. But they were, somehow . . . buttoned down. Quiet."

"But at that time, didn't you hate the war?"

"Oh. I did. You know that. I still do hate it. I hate what it did to us all." Ma sounds so sad. That's not the feeling I want now.

"But back then . . ." I prod.

Ma pauses. "Like a lot of people, I was mad at the guys who came back from Vietnam. I didn't realize how tough they had it. I thought *war, bad. Soldiers, bad,* like it was so simple, you know? I wanted to prove my own point of view." She laughs a little but with no happiness. "Things are more complicated than that. Now I know exactly how hard it was for them. What they had inside that they were trying to keep hold of. And the hurt they feel, it never goes away."

Could it be true, that something could harm you so much, so deep, it would *never* stop? My mind veers away from the thought of a hurt that goes on forever. Is everybody carrying around hidden pain that doesn't stop, pain we don't see? And did going to Trilby's funeral pull a hidden hurt out of Daddy, and put it on his surface?

But this is supposed to be a happy story. "So you challenged them to a game of pool."

"Yes. They teased me. Only your dad took me up on it."

"And you beat him," I say.

"I surely did. Which was a full miracle, because I wasn't good at pool."

"And then what?"

Her breath rises and falls. "He looked so bewildered. Lost."

"So you gave him a hug?"

"Yes, I did."

"And Daddy always says: *Your ma was the only woman ever fit just right in my arms.*"

"Yes. That's what he always says."

But he does not always say it, not anymore. We both know it, and knowing drains all the love from the story and turns it into hurt again.

Daddy does not come home.

CHAPTER ELEVEN

7:15 in the morning.

Me and Lady are on our way to school to meet with Pastor Jinks. We drive in thick silence. Me holding my breath against her My Sin perfume. Her pink fingernails *tap, tapping* on the steering wheel.

Daddy is not coming to the meeting.

Daddy did not get home.

At 7:35 Pastor Jinks pours coffee for Lady. Ever since we got here, Lady and the pastor have done nothing but exchange small talk about the beautiful weather and last Sunday's moving church sermon.

At last, the pastor gets to the point. "Mrs. Hawkins," he says. "I'm sorry not to see Lyndie's father. I was looking forward to meeting him."

"He sends his regrets," Lady says smoothly. "He had an important appointment this morning."

I stare at Lady.

"The thing is," the pastor says, "I'd like to be of help."

Lady's shoulders stiffen. Lady needs no *help*. Not from Mrs. Spurlock, not from Pastor Jinks. Not from anybody. And don't I know it.

"I don't mean to pry," he says. "But, if there's some complication in the household . . ."

"Complication." Lady says the word like it is laced with poison.

"What I mean is—" The pastor sends me a warm look. "My impression is that Lyndie is feeling a little anxious."

"I see." Lady grasps my wrist in her gloved hand. "It's a confusing age, eleven years old. You're neither one thing nor another. In my day, we called it growing pains."

"She's had a lot to absorb, moving to a new home," Pastor Jinks adds. "As Lyndie and I touched on yesterday, you might consider arranging for her to speak to a children's counselor." His voice is soothing. "Sometimes, it's easier for young people to open up with an outsider. We families get so close, we can't see each other fully."

When Pastor Jinks says "counselor," Lady does something with her mouth that looks like she inhaled a bug. The atmosphere in Pastor Jinks's cramped study is suddenly very tense.

The pastor turns to me in a friendly way. "Could that be, Lyndie?"

I sit there gulping. Knocking my knees together under my wool skirt.

"Especially if Lyndie's mother is unwell," he says. "My own mother became very ill, when I was a teenager." Pastor Jinks's eyes are full of sympathy. "I—I worried about my mama night and day."

"Pastor," Lady says, "Lyndie's mother occasionally suffers mild headaches. Rest assured, we have no *complications* in our household."

Lady is going to kill me for telling the pastor any single thing about us. Please, please, Pastor Jinks. Do not mention Daddy again.

"I don't believe Lyndie, or anyone else in my family, needs a counselor, Pastor." Lady's cheeks are mottling red under her makeup. "I understood we were here to discuss Lyndie's truancy."

"Yes. I don't mean to pry."

"There are no difficulties at home." Lady sets down her coffee cup and draws herself up. "We have always been a vigorous family," she says. "On both sides. Ever since the day my husband's grandfather Fayette Hawkins became first county judge in Greeneville, Tennessee. As for my own people, they are cut from the same bolt of cloth. You may know, my daughter, Palm Rae, is married to the Mayor of Bryson City, North Carolina."

"Your distinguished families are certainly an asset to their communities," says the pastor.

Lady turns my wrist loose.

"My son was laid off from his job last spring," Lady says, shocking me out of my fidgets. "That's no secret, and no shame. Every cloud has a silver lining. Tad and I are overjoyed to have our whole family together under one roof."

"Of course you are."

I bet Pastor Jinks believes he might get Lady to open up and confide in him, like he does everyone else. But Lady does not "confide" in outsiders. I stare out the gritty window, suddenly lightheaded. When I glance at Lady, she is looking at me like a cat with her eye fixed on a lizard. I am so dead.

"Indeed," she says. "Tyrus has some excellent prospects. He is examining his options."

"That's good to hear, Mrs. Hawkins. It's hard for veterans, especially if they don't have something meaningful to keep them productive. The wounds from that war never quite heal. Best we can do is help them keep the bandages on."

The hurt never really goes away. That's what Ma said.

"Thank heavens, we have no worries in that department." Lady is so cool, butter wouldn't melt in her mouth.

A slow, bubbling confusion makes me shift in my chair. How can she *lie* like this when Daddy has gone missing? Or did Ma make up some excuse for Daddy being away, and Lady thinks she's telling the truth now? Or *is* Lady telling the truth, and Daddy really went to Knoxville on business?

"At any rate—" Pastor Jinks smiles at me. "Lyndie has promised she will come to school every day now."

"I apologize for any inconvenience Lyndie caused you." Lady rises, brushing an invisible speck of lint from her lapel. "My granddaughter"—she pins me with a look that freezes my bones—"has been disciplined."

"No inconvenience, Mrs. Hawkins." The pastor gets up too. "I'm very fond of Lyndie. Feel free to call on me. I'm always here to help."

There's that word again. *Help*. Help that we Hawkinses never, ever need according to Lady.

In the hall outside the front office, Lady hisses at me. "You and I have a bone to pick. I'll come get you when school lets out. Be outside at two thirty-five sharp."

I climb the stairs to second period Advanced English. Before class starts, D.B. is passing around a sign-up sheet. "Kickboxing club," he tells each person. "Seven a.m. to seven thirty on Mondays before school. We'll be meeting in the quad." But all the kids shake their heads, looking at him funny—this pudgy new boy in his baggy uniform, supposedly a juvenile delinquent, who wants to start his own club. "No can do," says Jarrod Pierce. "Football practice."

"As if," Hillary Baggett sniffs. She counts off on her fingers. "Bible theater club, piano. And I've got riding lessons twice a week."

Me and Dawn are sitting at our grouped desks, figuring out next steps in our team project. Oral presentations on our partners happen next week. Dawn is reading over the answers on my icebreaker sheet. "Are you planning to use any photos or visuals for your presentation?"

"Nah," I say.

"Don't you think you should?"

"I guess that means you think I should. Why don't you say so."

"What's wrong?"

"I don't constantly need your *help*, Dawn. You're like always there with all kinds of advice I didn't ask for. I think

I can figure this presentation out on my own. This is not rocket science."

Dawn flushes. "We're supposed to be working as a team."

"Well, I'm a team of one now, okay? So back off."

"You can't really be a team of one," Dawn mutters. "I don't know what you have to be so ugly about."

This is true. She doesn't know what I have to be so ugly about. Because: 1) She can't keep a secret, and 2) She's too relentlessly sunny-side-up to ever begin to think about anything sad.

But there's something I need to know that only Dawn can tell me, so I look around to make sure nobody can hear, and lean close to her. "Dawn," I say in a low voice.

"What?"

"Are you Spurlocks planning to keep D.B. with you, like, until twelfth grade?"

Dawn's mouth turns down. "He's on Trial Release. He's only allowed to live with us for one school year."

"How long does he have to be at Pure Visions? He said if he makes straight A's this year, he can get out."

Dawn shakes her head. "He's in there until he's eighteen."

This really throws me. Is it possible D.B. really doesn't know that? That all his hard work and hoping and good behavior won't amount to a hill of beans?

"But what if his foster mom wanted him?"

"If you don't mind, I don't really want to talk to you now." Dawn tosses her bangs.

"He said the fire was an accident."

She sighs and drops her pencil. Dawn can't resist discussing her charity case. "Kids were playing with a lighter in his closet. But he got tried for arson. There's consequences."

"He's only twelve. He deserves to be free."

"He can't get out," Dawn says. "What's it to you, anyway?"

D.B. comes over and we both hush on this subject.

"I'm sorry I can't do kickboxing club, D.B. I have Math Maniacs and dance class, and I still have to get all my knitting done for Holiday Hats for the Homeless. My hats are not going so great." She's completely freezing me out now. She pulls a handful of hat rejects out of her knitting bag.

"Well, they look mostly warm anyway," D.B. says. "Except for the gaping holes."

"If something opens up, I'll come for certain."

"Sorry, I can't," I tell him. "I'm grounded. Plus, Lady would unzip me up one side and down the other if I started kickboxing. I might as well tattoo cuss words on my forehead."

D.B. goes around to every single person in class with that sign-up sheet. PeeWee, who is being a gigantic pill, yanks his desk away from our team and moves it behind us.

When D.B. offers him the sign-up sheet, he laughs in his face. "You a kickboxer, fatty? Yeah, I'm *so sure*."

D.B. takes his seat and stares ahead. "Fine," he mutters. "There is one person in my club. Me."

"You are in the category of lonesome kickboxers," I say. "Which is kind of romantic, if you think about it. Like a lonesome cowboy, right? But hey, if Lady lets me off the hook next week, I'll join your club. It sounds like exactly what I want to do right now. How do you know how to kickbox, anyway?"

"My foster dad was teaching me some," D.B. says. "I also maybe have a blood uncle somewhere who was a champion. The Screaming Eagle, I think they called him. I bet he was really tough."

Screaming Eagle. I like the sound of that—it has *narrative* potential. I scribble the name down on a piece of paper.

Mrs. Flannigan arrives, and we get down to a lesson about Types of Conflict in Literature.

Human against Animal, Mrs. Flannigan is writing on the chalkboard.

"Can someone give me an example?" Mrs. Flannigan says. I don't raise my hand.

Lady against Velvet the deer.

Lady against Hoopdee.

Lady against the mice under the house.

Dawn pipes up, "The movie *Jaws*?"

"That's an excellent example."

Behind me, PeeWee starts humming the *Jaws* theme music of an approaching shark. *Bum,* bum. *Bum,* bum. Jarrod Pierce takes up the theme. The class is starting to giggle.

"How about, Human against Nature?" Mrs. Flannigan asks.

Union and Confederate soldiers against measles, chicken pox, scurvy, dysentery.

"*Robinson Crusoe*?" Hillary calls out.

"Yes, Hillary. Good."

The sawing shark music starts up again with renewed enthusiasm.

Bumbum bumbum bumbumbumbum.

I crane around and give PeeWee and Jarrod the stink eye. "Will you please shut up? That is totally distracting."

PeeWee snaps his gum at me. "*You* shut up."

"Oh, yeah?"

"Lyndie, turn around, please," Mrs. Flannigan says. "How about Human against Human?"

Me against PeeWee.

Me against Lady.

A sharp tug on my braid snaps my head back. I whip

around again. PeeWee Bliss's face is pink with laughter. A mess of silver Wrigley's gum wrappers are scattered on his desk. He pulls a wad of gum out of his mouth and dangles it at me. Jarrod Pierce and Frank Stoppard look ready to bust up entirely. When I reach back to feel my braid, there's a huge wad of sticky between the woven strands.

"Are you *kidding* me?" I scream it out before I can even think. Mrs. Flannigan's hand pauses in midair. She has written on the chalkboard:

Antagonist.

This time, PeeWee has pushed me too far. I lunge from my desk.

"Hold on, Lyndie!" D.B. says. "You don't have to—"

But I'm already on top of PeeWee with my fists flailing.

PeeWee is howling like the lily-livered coward that he is, clutching his nose, and I hardly even got to punch him.

"You know where to go, Lyndon." Mrs. Flannigan points at the door. "PeeWee, get to the infirmary. Now. And tilt your head back. Don't you dare drip blood on my clean floor."

I keep my eyes down as I gather up my books. I'm at Pastor Jinks's door again before I can say *Human against Herself.*

After last bell, Lady's Cadillac is idling outside the front doors of Covenant, like she said. There's no getting around it. I have to climb in.

"This is the limit!" Lady fumes when we turn out of the parking lot. "Another call about your misbehavior, not two hours after our meeting this morning. Fighting in class! I have never been so humiliated in all my born days." Lady's gloved hands grip the steering wheel. "A *counselor,* he says. We do not go spilling our private business to head doctors— the very idea." She's so furious, she's hitting the gas and the brakes, speeding and slowing, jerking us around on the road.

Up on the ridge road, we almost mow over somebody's mailbox.

"Did Daddy come home?"

"He has business," Lady says. "In Knoxville. He'll be home when he's home."

"What kind of business," I say. "Ma didn't say he had business."

"That's not your concern."

"*Why* is Daddy in Knoxville?" I kick at the floorboards in frustration. "Nobody ever tells me the damn truth."

"Don't you dare use language with me. Stop that kicking right now. Do *you* tell the truth, Lyndie Hawkins? Do you? Or do you tell it only when it suits you?"

I stare out the window.

"Oh mercy," Lady says. "What did I do to be burdened with such a child? My sweet mother must be looking down from heaven and raining tears."

Here it comes again.

"Let's hope Great-Grandma keeps crying through the dry season," I say. "At least the carrots and green beans will stay watered."

"It will be all over town by nightfall that the pastor thinks my family needs psychiatric care. How could you be so disloyal?"

"I was not disloyal! I only said Ma had headaches. Besides, Pastor Jinks would never, ever say we are crazy. Anyhow, why do you care what other people think?"

"What other people think can cause more chaos and heartbreak than you will ever know." Spurlocks' white picket fence whizzes by in a blur. "Nosy do-gooders who can't mind their own business." She chokes on her words. "This is how families get broken. I've done everything I know how to do, to keep this family together."

"Well, good job," I say. "We couldn't be happier."

Lady's face blotches. But this road is narrow. She has to keep her eye on the turns.

"Promise me." Lady takes an unsteady breath. "That you will never, ever, *ever* discuss such things outside our family again. I have friends in this town, and believe you me, if you do, I will hear about it. And you will be grounded into next year."

"Like that's anything new," I mutter.

"Promise me, Lyndie!" Her voice cracks.

"Okay, okay, okay," I say. "I promise."

Outside the car window, rain clouds are gathering over the mountains. I would never admit it to Lady, but she does have a point. Telling people stuff about us Hawkinses has never resulted in anything but fights and teasing and trouble, for me personally.

CHAPTER TWELVE

He is nowhere.

Thursday, Friday, the grown-ups are all sunk into themselves and quiet; Ma at work or behind her wall of books, Grandpa Tad mostly at the office, Lady busy with History Museum tours. From early morning till school lets out, I can wall up my worry about Daddy with chores and classes. But once I'm home, his aftershave smell lingers on the bath towels, his denim shirt hangs on a hook, his *Newsweek* magazines lie scattered on the hall table.

Ma catches me on my way past her door as I come out of the bathroom on Saturday morning braiding up my clean-washed hair. I've finally got the last of PeeWee's chewing gum out, which is totally disgusting, using peanut butter and an old toothbrush.

"Lyndie," she says when I plop down on her bed. "I want you to finish unpacking your boxes today." There are still eight cardboard cartons stacked in the corner of my bedroom. Only one is open, spilling things I had no choice but to excavate: school uniforms, pajamas, my old stuffed bear, Teddy Roosevelt, who keeps me company at night now that Hoopdee can't.

She's not the only one nagging me to do this. Lady hits me up to finish unpacking about seventeen times per hour. I don't want to. Unpacking would only make going back to our real home more impossible.

"Where is Daddy?" I say. "When is he coming home?"

Ma sighs. "I don't know. Soon. Please stop asking."

"Maybe when he forgets *you* told him to get out," I say. "Fine." And slope off to my bedroom. My heart feels scoured out and I need some relief. My library books are still in those boxes somewhere. They're so far overdue now, I'll have to break into my coin bank to pay what I owe.

But:

Lady will drop Ma at work, then go to the museum. I bet I can convince Grandpa Tad to take me to Love's Forge Library. I'll return the books and ask Mrs. Dooley to help me research D.B.'s name, Dalzell, and also his maybe-uncle, the kickboxer named Screaming Eagle.

While I wait for them to leave, I pull down one particular box from the top of the heap, straining when the weight of it hits my arms. *Memorabilia and Books* it says in Magic Marker. I set it down and peel back the tape.

Before Ma made me throw everything together in a jumble, I organized this box careful. It's the one with my favorite things from Daddy. Like my prized Confederate Treasury Note for one hundred dollars, with the coal-fired train printed on the front that Daddy gave me for my ninth birthday. It'll be "worth a fortune someday," he said.

I dig around for my brass spyglass from 1860 that I got two years ago on our road trip to Alabama to visit Granny and Auntie Pearl.

On that trip, I begged Daddy to take us along the southern route of the Trail of Tears, where the Cherokees had to walk a thousand miles when they got removed by the U.S. Army. I read aloud to Ma and Daddy from my library book about how so many Cherokee people died along the way. We all got quiet while we drove after that. Mile after mile, I looked out the window through my telescope to try to keep focused and not cry imagining those Cherokee children and what it would feel like to be ripped away from your real home and forced to march to a new life in a strange place you never wanted.

Nobody in Love's Forge ever talks about the Trail of Tears.

In my memorabilia box, there's also a set of dominoes in a wood box—the dominoes are made of real animal bone. Another birthday present from Daddy. And an embossed powder flask that a soldier would have carried for when he loaded his gun, which Ma got annoyed with me for buying at a junk shop because she objects to weapons (a powder flask is not a weapon, obviously). And last thing, a gold-plated locket on a chain. I pull the locket out and pry it open. There are two yellowed round photographs, one on either side, of a black man and a black woman, the husband wearing a hat with a silk band, and the wife's picture smiling in his direction. Daddy and I bought this locket when we stopped to browse at Uncle Braxton's Americana Shoppe when we took a road trip to explore West Virginia last year.

They must have loved each other some, the couple in this locket. When I snap the locket closed, it's like they are caught in a private hug.

I bet the wife wore it on a chain, keeping it close to her heart. Did Ma and Daddy love each other so, ever? Yes, they surely did. Not even so long ago, they were still sharing jokes and holding hands. I'm stopped still, remembering, listening to the silence in this house. I'm listening for the sound of Daddy's voice teasing Lady. Or him phony-singing

Dolly Parton songs in a high falsetto while he shaves. Even his pacing—his boots on the floorboards—would make me feel better now.

Instead, what I do hear is Grandpa Tad making his way slowly downstairs, one *clump* at a time, from the grandparents' bedroom on the third floor. When he reaches the landing and passes my door, he pokes his head in.

"Hey, Lyndiebird, what've you got there?" He gestures at the locket.

"Nothing." I drop the locket back in the box, and start feeling around for my library books.

"You planning to put your things away? Or are you fixing to move out sometime soon?"

If only.

"I bet you could use some help." He glances around. "This room is lonely, and has been for years. But you can make it feel *lived* in," he says. "Rooms truly appreciate having a person to inhabit them."

He takes a couple of steps in. "Maybe it's a matter of getting started."

One hour later, me and Grandpa Tad have unpacked my clothes boxes and hung up all my shirts and pants and put folded things in the chest of drawers. That's the limit of all I would let us unpack.

We hear Lady's Cadillac pull out from the driveway. She and Ma will be gone all day now. Grandpa Tad looks out my bedroom window. He pushes his glasses up the bridge of his nose, his face broody. "We ought to replace that flag on the front gate," he says. "Looks like it's been through the Revolutionary War, and then some."

"Only, the American flag didn't have all those stars in the Revolution. Only thirteen."

"Do tell. I wonder when the first American flag was ever flown."

"The first American flag was raised in 1777," I say. "During the siege of Fort Stanwix in the Mohawk River Valley, in New York."

"Ah," says Grandpa Tad. "Fort Stanwix."

"The soldiers cut up their white shirts to make the stripes, and the red petticoats of their wives. They got the blue from a captain's coat."

"Whoa, now. I thought the first flag was made by Miss Betsy Ross."

"There is no historical evidence for that," I say. "That is a made-up story. Like George Washington and his cherry tree. Also not true."

"You don't say. How'd you get to know all this?"

"I read a lot. And Mrs. Dooley at the library, she helps

me figure things out." Which makes a fine transition to the first step of my plan. "Hey, Grandpa, do you think you could drive me to the library? I need to do research for a school project."

"Well now." Grandpa Tad turns, holding back a grin, and right then, I see Daddy in that wicked humorous glint in his eye. "Are you still grounded?"

"I guess so."

"I suppose we can slip on out to the library, long as we're home before your grandma. But you have to promise not to tell on me."

"I promise."

Grandpa Tad drops me at the library after lunch with a book bag full of overdue biographics.

Mrs. Dooley is leaning on her elbows at the front desk. "Long time no see, Lyndie Hawkins. You must have had a busy summer."

I unload a stack of biographies in front of her.

"And you must know everything anybody ever wanted to know about the Lincolns," Mrs. Dooley says. "Let's see how well you retain what you read. Tell me something I don't know."

"Fact," I say. "Mary Lincoln and Abraham Lincoln's best friends at one time were black people."

"Go on."

"Elizabeth Keckley was Mary Lincoln's best friend. She had been enslaved. And for Abe, his best friend was his bodyguard and valet, William H. Johnson, a free black man who died of typhoid fever—fever he might have caught from President Lincoln, but that is speculation." I count out a handful of quarters and dimes. Thinking how close the Lincolns were to their friends makes me feel in very short supply of my own best friend, Dawn Spurlock. Was I always just Lonely Little Lyndie to her?

"Very informative. Fact or fiction?" Mrs. Dooley says. "Lincoln fought the Civil War to free enslaved people, so they could become full American citizens."

I hesitate. That's a tough one, and it pains my heart, because I so admire President Lincoln. "I don't know," I admit. "It says in one of these books that for quite some time, Lincoln was saying enslaved people should definitely go free. But also that after the war, they should volunteer to leave the country, to go to colonies in Central America, or go back to Africa. Because he couldn't see them ever being equal in American society. Being allowed to vote and everything."

"Yes," Mrs. Dooley says. "Our heroes all have flaws and complications. They make mistakes. They are sometimes dead wrong. It's good to learn that sooner than later."

That reminds me why I'm here. "Mrs. Dooley, my English teacher thinks we need to write about more than our own selves for a change. Learn something serious about other people. Figure out their *narrative*."

Mrs. Dooley dumps my change into a drawer, then looks me over, her eyes sharp through her big square-framed glasses.

"I'm listening."

"We're supposed to be researching family history or cultural history of our partner. My partner doesn't have parents or a home, only an ex–foster mother now, but he thinks he might have an uncle somewhere, on his mom's side. Somebody called Screaming Eagle. Who is a kick-boxer."

"Screaming Eagle. When is this project due?"

"Next Thursday," I say. "I'm supposed to give a live presentation. I also want to look up where in Scotland my partner's name came from, *Dee-Ell*, spelled D-A-L-Z-E-L-L."

Mrs. Dooley takes me into a little dark alcove behind the stacks. "This is our microfilm room." She points to a humongous machine that's sort of like a cross between a personal TV and a slide projector. "You research newspaper stories here. Do you know where this . . . er . . . Screaming Eagle happens to come from?"

"Maybe Tennessee, maybe North Carolina. I'm not sure."

"You probably want to start with *The Tennessean* and then branch out to other states nearby. Try the *Raleigh News and Observer* next."

She shows me how to feed the long rolls of brown film into the machine. The film is covered with newspaper pages in miniature, any day in history you want, in tons of different newspapers, all the way back practically since newspapers were first invented.

Mrs. Dooley sets out rolls of microfilm in metal canisters. At first, I skim through sports pages of random editions from *The Tennessean* as fast as I can. But I realize if I really want to find Screaming Eagle, I'm going to have to slow down and pay attention. I may have to camp out in the microfilm room all day.

It takes hours to read through five years of the *Tennessean* sports pages. I finally turn to the *Raleigh News and Observer*. It gets to a point where the words don't even look like words anymore. By this time, though, I'm totally an

expert in the brutal ways of flying punches and cross counters, of hooking knee strikes and snap knee strikes. Also,
the inside story on dislocated jawbones. But I don't find any
articles about a fighter called Screaming Eagle.

My shoulders ache, but the ache revs up my stubborn-
ness. I read stories about boxers and kickboxers called
Homicide Hank and Gator Garland and Thunder Thur-
man, hoping for clues. Somewhere around hour three, Mrs.
Dooley checks in on me for the third time.

"You're going to get a crick in your neck, Lyndie. Enough
research for one day."

"A couple more minutes, please?" I'm skimming an article buried in the very back of the *Raleigh News* sports
pages. UNFINISHED BUSINESS! the headline blares. It's
an article sandwiched between batting averages and an ad-
vertisement for something called Elixir of Zeus that prom-
ises to make men more manly. I near about jump out of my
chair. There's a kickboxing match between a fighter named
Alonso Mad Dog Lopez vs. Mac Screaming Eagle Driver.
It says Screaming Eagle has come out of retirement for a
rematch.

"Found him!" I pump my fist at Mrs. Dooley. "This article
says Screaming Eagle Driver is going to fight Mad Dog
Lopez again in October!"

Before he retired, Screaming Eagle Driver was an undefeated welterweight who won twenty-eight fights in a row. He even won three back-to-back fights in one day. However, a short commentary reveals that he was suffering from bad diet and dehydration during his last fight, and came close to breaking his winning streak.

"Nice work," Mrs. Dooley says. She hands me a package of peanut butter crackers from the vending machine. "Press that red button if you want to print out your story," she says over her shoulder.

But when I look back at the date, the paper is from 1982. Three years ago! Ancient history. I don't even know how this fight ended.

But I'm getting a bigger idea. A better idea. A notion that is so much greater than anything to do with our class presentation.

What if I could find Mac Screaming Eagle Driver somehow? If it turns out he's really a blood relative to D.B., maybe he could help get D.B. away from Pure Visions?

I write down the newspaper date in my composition book, and the name of the journalist at the *Raleigh News* who wrote the article. I press a button that spits out a copy of the page. The photo of Screaming Eagle Driver is pretty grainy, but he looks to be made of muscle, with a face that never cracked a smile. I look hard for any resemblance to D.B., who is big and kind of wiggly, with a gap-toothed grin. I can't find any.

Poor D.B. He has no more biological parents, and his foster dad is dead. This Screaming Eagle definitely looks like one tough cookie. But I guess when it comes to family, you don't get to pick and choose.

I roll up the microfilm, stick it back in its tin canister. I'm still blinking in the bright light of the library, and my whole body is fizzy with excitement, when I see Mrs. Dooley up on a ladder sorting thick encyclopedias in the medical section by the front door.

She climbs down and points to a book on the nearest table. "That's a history of the Scottish clans," she says. "You can take this home to look for the Dalzell name."

"Perfect." I load the book into my bag. "Can we check on something for my science class now? I need to find out what causes people to have hand tremors."

"Is that so?" Mrs. Dooley regards me narrowly. "I recall that seventh-grade science at Covenant is focused on the life cycle of mosses and ferns this time of year. Has that changed?" She points at the glass door. "Your grandfather is here." Grandpa Tad is starting haltingly up the front steps, come to fetch me. My Cinderella watch tells me it's

3:40. Lady will be heading home soon. We have to beat her there, or I'll be grounded until Christmas.

"Go on out now," Mrs. Dooley says. "Don't make your grandfather climb up all those stairs."

"Okay. Thanks, Mrs. Dooley." I yank open the library door and run down to meet him.

CHAPTER THIRTEEN

By Tuesday, there's still no sign of Daddy. He's been gone seven days, a full week. The missing him has started to eat away at my brain. I only have two more days to get my presentation for Advanced English ready, and I can't hardly concentrate.

When I get home after school, the house is silent. Which is happening a lot lately. Mail is scattered on the hall table like somebody threw it down in a hurry, and the hall closet is partway open. Lady's Cadillac is gone; she's probably at the museum. Ma's day off is Tuesday, so I guess she's asleep. I wriggle out of my plaid skirt and stiff blouse and I'm pulling on a pair of jeans when the phone rings.

I sprint downstairs to pick up the phone, thinking— *Daddy. Maybe he's calling!*

"Yo," D.B. says when I answer, and I feel myself deflate.

"Can you come over to Spurlocks'? To work on our English project. Mrs. Spurlock wants to know if you're free to have supper with us."

Mrs. Spurlock wants to know. Not *Dawn* wants to know.

"I'm not free at all. I have not one ounce of freedom. I told you, I'm grounded. I'm not allowed off the property."

Plus, who wants a Spurlock charity meal?

"But we have to work on our presentation! It's the day after tomorrow!"

"If you come up to the gate we can talk over it," I say. "That's about the best I can do."

"Are there snacks?"

"I know they feed you at Spurlocks'."

"They do. But no snackety snacks between meals. I'm, you know, peckish."

"*Peckish* is not a word."

"Yeah it is, I looked it up. It means *disposed to peck*."

"Like a chicken?"

"You got it."

"I can probably find you some food. Meet me at the gate in ten."

In the kitchen, rifling through the pantry, I remember something D.B. told me. About his grandmother's sugar and butter sandwiches. Heck, why not?

There's soft butter on the counter, a bag of white sugar in the pantry, a new loaf of Wonder Bread in the breadbox. I make two sandwiches and wrap them in waxed paper.

I meet D.B. at our front gate. "Here, peck on these." I hand him the sandwiches and lean my elbows on the gate rails. Grandpa Tad was right: The American flag strung up on the gate does look dim and tattered.

"You should see PeeWee's face," D.B. says. "He's down at Spurlocks' now. You have a heck of a punch. I guess you've had lots of practice."

"What's that supposed to mean?"

"Dawn says you used to get in fights all the time."

"Yeah. But mostly with PeeWee."

D.B. unwraps a sandwich and bites into it. "Whoa," he says. He closes his eyes, chewing slowly. "I haven't had one of these in, like, forever!"

"You're welcome." His expression is pure bliss. At least making D.B. happy is one thing I can fix right.

He says through a mouthful of bread and sugar, "PeeWee has his nose taped up. It's broken."

"I shouldn't ought to have hit him. Pastor Jinks says I need to develop impulse control. He says violence is not an effective way to resolve conflict."

"Better tell that to the rest of humankind," D.B. says.

"However, martial arts club could help with your impulse control. Not that I'm hinting or anything."

"I can't see how more fighting would result in less fighting."

D.B. splits the second sugar sandwich down the middle and hands me half. "It's a paradox." He licks butter off his thumb. "English vocab word."

Our eyes meet. His eyelashes are ridiculously long.

"Your eyes are different colors."

"Heterochromia," he says. "That would be a good detail to write down about me, by the way. For your presentation."

I nibble my half sandwich. "This is sort of yummy, actually. In a gross kind of way."

I wipe buttery hands on my jeans and prop my binder on the fence, flipping to the section for Advanced English. "You sure know a lot of vocab for someone who doesn't read."

D.B. pulls his notebook out of his backpack. "I've been doing an insanely impressive amount of studying. I'm two full years behind in math. I have to get on grade level by Christmas. I need to make straight A's. To convince the judge I should be in a good school. Dawn is tutoring me."

"But hardly anybody makes all A's at Covenant. You might want to reach for a lower star."

Determination shines from D.B.'s two-color eyes, but his chin trembles. "I have to be *perfect* this year. I can't get in any trouble."

"But, if you don't go back to Pure Visions, where would you live?"

"Don't know." He's picking at the white paint on our gate, flaking it off. "I could find my uncle, Screaming Eagle. Maybe he'd take me in." All the cheerfulness has drained from his face.

"Oh. But where are your real parents?"

"Is that question on the worksheet? Besides, what's a *real* parent?" He looks past me.

I scan down the icebreaker worksheet. All the questions I'm dying to ask D.B. aren't on it. *What does it feel like to have no parents? No true home?*

"After my biological dad died, I went to live with my grandma. Mom couldn't take care of me alone with no job. When Grandma got too sick to have me there, Mom dropped me off at a hospital. With all my clothes and a couple of toys in a garbage bag." D.B. mimes throwing a garbage bag over his shoulder, like a hobo. "I was seven." He's not smiling. "Nobody ever found out what happened to my mom, after."

"Oh gosh."

"Anyway, none of that goes in your presentation," he

says abruptly. "Here's what I think. To find out the truth about you, I've got to see how you live."

I glance back at Lady and Grandpa Tad's farmhouse.

"Like, for example," D.B. says, "if you took me on a tour of the Hawkins house, I bet I could really rock my presentation. A-plus in the bag."

"This isn't my real house. It isn't going to tell you a thing about me."

D.B. climbs up the gate and hovers over the top post. He stretches out a tentative leg. "What happens when I put my foot down on Hawkins property? Do I turn into a toad?"

"The opposite. You turn back from a toad into a handsome prince."

"Works for me."

We start at the top of the house and make our way down.

Lady and Grandpa Tad's room is on the third floor. I haven't been up here since I was little. Grandpa's side of the bedroom has law books and diplomas on a shelf. There's a picture of Daddy with Aunt Palm Rae when she was twelve and he was ten, with a crooked smile, several cowlicks, and all-over freckles.

Lady's side is floral. On her nightstand, an appointment

book is open to today's date. That's it. Plus a clock with frolicking angels. I peer over her appointment book. She's got a schedule for herself practically a twin of the one she made for me. I scan down past the museum tours and the household chores. At 7:45 p.m. she has written: *Time with Lyndie (Tea and Cookies)*. And drawn a star there.

Torture Lyndie would be more truthful.

"Who's in the picture?" D.B. points to the painting above the nightstand.

"That's Lady's mama, my great-grandma Waldrop. She painted her own portrait."

"That's very, um, interesting. If you like black and purple."

"They say she was high-strung. Now she just rains down tears from heaven over my bad behavior."

D.B. cocks an eyebrow. "You're bad?"

"So my grandma says."

"That's something we have in common." He gapes around. "Wow. This room looks like two animals from separate species live in it."

He writes something in his notebook. In my grandparents' bathroom, their water glasses sit side by side, where they put their teeth at night. Grandpa Tad's extra bridge is floating in one glass like a science experiment, pink and lifelike. "Separate species that wear false teeth," I observe.

But I sort of like the idea of my grandparents' separate teeth floating there, side by side in the darkness. It reminds me how I came up one night a long time ago, when I was staying over for the weekend. Grandpa Tad and Lady were asleep, still holding hands between their two twin beds.

"How come, would you *speculate*—that's a vocab word—the separate species got married?" D.B. says.

"Grandpa Tad says Lady loved him on account of he was a super-good lawyer. Having a man who knew how to win made her feel like, no matter what happened, she could always get out of a jam."

"So have you?"

"Have we what?" I'm leafing through Lady's appointment book. Every day looks basically the same. Then I turn a page and see the airmail letter tucked in there.

"Gotten out of a jam."

"Oh. We haven't had to get out of any jams. Grandpa has gotten lots of *other* people out of jams. Lady says he could argue his way out of a straightjacket inside a locked trunk. He's won 98.6 percent of his cases." The ink on the outside of the airmail letter is faded. It's addressed to Lady. When I unfold it, I know Daddy's handwriting. The date at the top says October 17, 1970. Fifteen years ago. *Dear Mama,* it says on the brittle blue paper.

Viet Nam is a more beautiful place than
anybody ever heard of, a place of Heaven
and Hell on earth, mountains, swamps, rice
paddies, sand, jungles full of tigers and men
who want to kill me. How many friends must
I see die before I get home to my family?

I read the letter again. Then I close it up and tuck it back inside Lady's book. She would ground me until doomsday if she caught me snooping. But the words go round in my head. Like one of Trilby's poems, maybe.

Jungles full of tigers
Men who want to kill me
How many friends must I see die . . .

It's like the letters of the Civil War that soldiers wrote with berry ink. Like one I read from a Union major, Sullivan Ballou. He wrote, *Death is creeping behind me with his fatal dart* on the night before a big battle. As if he knew he would surely die. I'd read that letter so many times, my heart heavy, I almost had it memorized.

How hard it is for me to burn to ashes the

hopes of future years, when, God willing, we might still have lived and loved together, and seen our boys grow up to honorable manhood around us.

Major Ballou never came home.

D.B. follows me downstairs.

"Can I ask a harder question?" D.B. is swinging on the banisters, taking two steps at a time.

"Yes. But quietly. Ma is most likely asleep." I point to her closed door down the hall.

"Dawn wants to know if you are okay," D.B. whispers. "Moving away from your home and everything. The Spurlocks worry about you, you know? Dawn—"

"Why would they worry about me? There's nothing wrong with me. I don't need anybody worrying about me."

"Okay, okay. Geez." He trails me into Daddy's room.

"I'm not a charity case."

"Like me, you mean?"

"That's not—"

"I think you're *lucky* to live here. You have this cool house, and two whole parents, and two whole grandparents."

"That is a big surplus of grown-ups, you might notice."

D.B. goggles around. "I don't see any grown-ups."

142

"I doubt you'll keep thinking I'm so lucky, once you meet Lady Hawkins."

"Well, at least you have a place to call home."

I snort. On Daddy's dresser, there's a bowl of coins, my last year's school picture, and a photo of Daddy with some of his army buddies sitting on a wall of sandbags, smoking. Some are smiling. Some are looking straight at the camera with serious expressions. Everything in the picture, from their uniforms to the sandbags to the trees and rocks in the background, looks the same dusty color of gray.

Daddy's ring is on the dresser. It says *United States Army,* gold filigree around a red stone. Lots of men in this town came home from Vietnam wearing gold rings. PeeWee Bliss's dad in a casket, and Hillary Baggett's dad, who has to walk with two canes. Mr. Bushyhead, who rents a one-room apartment all by himself. And homeless Bernadette, who mostly stays under the bridge, her only brother got killed in the war. All hoping to save the world. And the world, far as I can tell, was not saved.

D.B. picks up the picture of Daddy with his army buddies. "My foster dad had a picture like this. Sandbags and everything."

"He was in Vietnam?"

"Yeah. Army. He was such a cool guy. He was half

Cherokee and he was teaching me all about his culture and Cherokee history. From, like, ancient stuff, all the way back to the Ice Age. We rode dirt bikes and raised puppies, and he got me interested in 4-H club. He's how I started learning martial arts. But the most important thing was"—D.B. turns away from me and squints out the window—"he told me I had an invincible purpose. That my purpose was stuck to me like a shadow. Even if I couldn't always see it, I had to wait for the right light to fall, and it would reveal itself."

"Did the right light fall yet?"

"I'm waiting."

D.B. puts the photo back on Daddy's dresser, carefully. "I thought my foster dad was solid as a rock. He wasn't."

I think about that. "I get what you mean." Daddy is seven days gone. D.B. is so open about his own hardships. I feel he would understand if I told him.

"I'd do anything to take back messing around with that lighter," D.B. says. "It was so, so, stupid."

"But, didn't your foster parents want to keep you, after the fire?"

D.B.'s eyes flicker toward me. "They already had trouble, I guess. My foster dad killed himself. Eleven months after I got sent to Pure Visions."

I think of Trilby Bigwitch's funeral. The terrible thing Trilby did. *Such a terrible thing. Well, bless him, Trilby is free now. He's out of pain,* the lady behind me had whispered.

I understand now. Trilby must have killed himself too. "Do you know why your foster dad, why he did it?" I say carefully.

D.B.'s Adam's apple moves when he swallows. "I hope it wasn't because of me," he says.

I keep quiet and wait. Ma says sometimes "being present" is all a person needs when they're upset.

"Please don't talk about that part when you give your presentation on me."

"I would never."

Outside Daddy's bedroom window, the sun is setting over the hills, throwing shadows across the driveway. D.B. turns toward the door. "I'd better get back."

"I guess we're as ready for our presentation now as we'll ever be." I walk him out to the gate. A cold wind is blowing. I pull my sweatshirt hood up. "You know what?" I say.

He's been so honest. This is a person who is not afraid to tell the truth. I'm on the verge of spilling everything, about Daddy's gun, and Ma screaming at him to *get out*. How Daddy has left us for a week now. How something changed after Trilby's funeral. Even though I promised Lady I wouldn't.

"My dad," I begin. I turn Daddy's army ring around and around on my thumb.

"Yeah?"

"My dad has no job," I blurt out, finally. "That's why we had to come live here." Each one of those words hurts, but at the same time, makes me feel a tiny bit free.

D.B. gives me a nudge. "Don't worry," he says. "I won't put that in my presentation."

CHAPTER FOURTEEN

After D.B. leaves, I run to the kitchen and grab the phone. I dial 411 for information. There's one more thing I want to do to get ready for Thursday.

"Information?"

"I need the phone number for the *Raleigh News and Observer*, please," I tell the operator.

She gives me the number and I write it down in my notes. I have one more loose end to tie up about D.B. I have to talk to the guy at the *Raleigh News* who wrote about Screaming Eagle.

When the parlor clock strikes six thirty, Grandpa Tad and Lady are still not home. Which totally defies all strict

Hawkins schedules. I've fed the animals, done my home-work, including adding a *huge* surprise to my presenta-tion on D.B., watered the ferns, and even cleaned out the awful mousetraps, which required a lot of bravery. By now, supper-making should be in progress. Come to think of it, I haven't heard Ma stirring either. She should be moving around, getting ready to come downstairs for supper.

I fly up the steps to the second floor and rap on Ma's door.

No answer.

"Ma?"

Not a peep.

When I push open her door, her bed is empty.

I'm here alone? Suddenly, the house feels too big, too dark, and too drafty. Where would Ma be? Somewhere with Lady? I jump down the stairs again. In the front hall, that scattered mail is not like Lady; she's such a fusspot about everything staying neat. She wouldn't leave the hall closet door ajar either. Something has happened.

I hurry around and turn on all the parlor lamps.

Hoopdee scritch-scratches at the front screen door. He hasn't gotten used to being kept outside. When I open the door, he's wagging and wiggling at me. Velvet is picking at weeds near the front porch.

"Hoopdee, where is everybody?" But he only shudders

and yawns. So I join them on the porch steps, elbows propped on my knees, shivering. Watching Velvet graze reminds me I'm supposed to turn her loose in another week. With Daddy absent, how will I be able to let one more thing go?

Hoopdee and me both stare down the drive. I decide to play Categories with Hoopdee to stop my brain from sounding over and over: *Where are they? Where are they? Where are they?*

"Hoopdee, you and me are in the category of Hawkinses who are both hungry and here," I tell him. "A category of lonely, worried, hungry Hawkinses who are here."

Dawn came up with Categories. One Saturday, back in my real home two years ago, we climbed up into the tree house with a sack of Cokes and individual-size bags of Fritos, along with the burnt rejects of brownies Dawn had baked for Hungry Honeys, her charity project. We played Categories to decide which people Dawn would deliver brownies to, in descending order. People who were both *hungry* and *sweet* were top category. Then people only hungry. Then people only sweet. Then the larger pool of people Dawn wanted to give brownies to, for various reasons, who were neither hungry nor particularly sweet, but if there were brownies left, would get some.

I never totally got the Spurlocks' devotion to their charity projects. I thought family should come first. Why spend all that energy giving things to people you hardly know, and who half the time don't even appreciate all the effort you put into it?

But Dawn glowed when she talked about Hungry Honeys.

She glowed when she talked about me too. *Lyndie is the best. She has the coolest mom and the coolest dad. Lives with the sweetest grandparents.* D.B. told me she said that.

That day in the tree house, me and Dawn were debating about her mailman, Mr. D'Onofrio, who was so big you wondered how they found a post office uniform to fit him. Dawn proposed that with a belly like that, Mr. D'Onofrio couldn't possibly be hungry, he must have recently finished chowing on something. I argued back that, having to keep such a big belly full, he was probably ravenous all the time. The one thing we agreed on was that Mr. D'Onofrio, who smelled of cigars and was inexplicably angry at cats, was not sweet.

Dawn had on a T-shirt with two pictures of Jesus facing in opposite directions, and the year, 1983, in swirly pink script with glitter, because she had gone to ScriptureLand the weekend before and ridden on the Holy Rollercoaster, which opened that month.

I unwrapped our burnt brownies, the ones Dawn had thrown into the no-way-are-we-feeding-these-to-needy-people pile.

"Wait, no," I said when she reached for one. "We need to figure out what category *you* go into." Dawn put down the bag of Fritos she had dug into, with a concerned look.

"You couldn't be hungry," I said. "That stack of waffles you ate at breakfast had to be a record."

"Your mom knows how much I love blueberry waffles," Dawn agreed. She still had blueberry stains around the corners of her mouth.

"I think you are not so much hungry, as you are kindhearted, which is a subcategory of sweet. You didn't want to hurt Ma's feelings eating only one waffle. So you ate four to make her happy."

"*I* think people who are hungry and kindhearted should be a separate category. A higher category than simply sweet and hungry."

"I believe you're right. Kindhearted is more specific." I nibbled one corner of a seriously charred brownie. "But it's sad for you to have to be in a category all by yourself," I said.

"Yes," Dawn agreed. "It's lonely at the top. But if you made yourself a little more kindhearted, you could join me."

"Okay." I handed her a brownie. "Please note how I generously gave you the brownie that is least burnt. That was very kindhearted of me."

"You'll get there, Lyndie." Dawn put a Frito on one corner of her brownie and bit into it happily. "I have faith in you."

It occurs to me that two years later, I haven't made too much progress on the kindheartedness. But Dawn said she had faith in me. Isn't having faith in somebody in the category of true friendship?

At seven p.m. by my Cinderella watch, it's full dark. I'm starting to bed down Hoopdee and Velvet in the barn when Lady's Cadillac turns past the American flag at the gate, with the Blue Bullet following behind. I blink in the glare of headlights. When the Cadillac pulls past, I see Grandpa Tad driving. Ma is at the wheel of the Blue Bullet.

I go crashing out the barn door, Hoopdee at my heels, already spitting questions and complaints.

But Grandpa Tad's face is grim when he climbs out.

"Get on inside the house, Lyndie," he says.

His tone of voice makes me back up, but I don't go in. I stand gaping while Ma comes around the side of the Blue

Bullet and Lady and Tad pull a person out of the backseat of the Cadillac, each holding an arm.

He is pale and slack-jawed and red-eyed. His clothes are a filthy mess, torn at the elbow and knee and a brown stain down the front of his blue shirt. Knuckles like he scraped them along a gravel path. I can smell him from here. Like he's been sleeping underground.

Light should be pouring into me. There are tickertape parades for returning soldiers, kisses and dances when wars are finally over. But looking at his scraggly beard, the scratches etched on his cheek, I want to cry.

"Daddy?" I croak out. "What happened?"

"Go inside. Into the parlor and shut the door, Lyndie," Lady says. "Now."

Hoopdee is all a-quiver, ears perked, tail thumping on anything it can thump, circling around their legs. He's the only one who looks partway happy.

I stare at this man, trying to overlay his beaten empty face with a face I remember from before last Tuesday. How has he come to change so much? My father keeps his trousers sharp-creased and smells like Aqua Velva. Now he looks like—like Hoopdee did, the day Daddy brought him home, all mangy and limping from his long wandering. Sick and exhausted and hopeless and homeless. A stray.

Daddy lifts his gaze as if to see me, but his eyes slide over the top of my head. "I can walk fine." Daddy shrugs Lady and Ma off. But he can't. He's got a limp in his right foot, his energy is drained out. I follow them inside, trying to get close.

Grandpa Tad pulls his hat off and throws it on the hall chair on top of my schoolbag.

Lady waves a hand at Ma. "Rainbow, will you put a kettle on? Lyndie, get to the parlor."

Ma gives me a quick squeeze before she hurries off to the kitchen. "It's okay," she whispers, but it's her lying voice. Grandpa Tad has Daddy by the arm. They start upstairs.

"Wait." I head after them, tug on Daddy's sleeve. "Is your leg hurt? What happened to his leg, Grandpa Tad? Daddy? Where *were* you?" What I wonder most is, *How could you leave like that? For so long, with not even a phone call?*

Now Lady comes after me, grabbing my arm hard, tearing me away from Daddy. Her face is all bunched up. She says through gritted teeth: "Hold your tongue, for once in your life. Do as you're told!"

I struggle out of her grasp. "Stop telling me what to do! I'm sick of you!" I yell into her face. "I hate it here! We all hate it here!"

Lady winces. She draws back to slap my face. But she collects herself at the last minute and drops her hand.

"This is your fault," I spit at her. "Daddy was fine until we came here. We were happy."

"Was he fine?" Lady cries. "You stupid child. Get into the parlor and close the door." Grandpa Tad and Daddy have made it to the second floor, and Grandpa is practically shoving Daddy down the hallway. Ma rushes out from the kitchen holding the teakettle.

Everything bad happened since we moved here. The whiskey and the gun. Ma telling him to *get out.*

Now my legs move in their own direction. Straight out the door of this choking dim house.

"Honey—" Ma says.

But I'm already pelting down the purple hill and onto the moonlit path through the woods, jumping tree roots and scratching my bare arms on branches, scattering pieces of my heart behind me as I run. Until at last I'm standing on wobbling legs, breathing hard, peering through a thicket hedge at the Spurlocks' little whitewashed stone cottage.

Dawn's laughter drifts over to me. I can make out the Spurlock twins in the light from the big fire they have lit, Dawn's little brothers Pitch and Paulson, and PeeWee Bliss is still there too. Dawn's flop-eared bunnies are out on the lawn. And D.B.'s voice, he's calling out, "One, two, three . . ." They're all creeping across the lawn toward D.B.'s turned back, and everybody except the bunnies freezes when he yells, "Statues!"

I was invited. I could have been here if Lady hadn't grounded me. There's the early evening sound of parents' voices, the screen door slamming and the smell of burgers and hot dogs on the grill. And I think, there is never such happy easy evening play in Grandpa and Lady's house, never a game spinning out in the cool front yard in the soft grass, never the smell of smoke and the promise of hot dogs on the grill and potato salad to come soon. I peer through the hedge, and Dawn and PeeWee are crouched frozen on the lawn trying to be statues, and the little brothers wriggle and groan and can't keep still for anything. Dawn's bunnies startle each other, jump up with a shiver, and take off in a mad chase.

Then D.B. does a jump and a hop and a spin and a round-house kick, like a real boxer, not for any reason but for the fun of it. He's like those bunnies, happy and completely free. The movement of his big body is so graceful. But me, I'm a frozen statue myself. I can't simply go out into the yard to join in, and say *hey*. And I can't go home, either.

I am in a category of one.

CHAPTER FIFTEEN

When I get home, it's near eight o'clock.

No supper on the table. Lady's in the kitchen on the phone. Two trays of tomato soup and saltine crackers are on the counter.

"My goodness, who told you that?" she says into the phone. "Disorderly conduct? Oh my Lord, no." She lets loose a tinkle of laughter. "My son was not *arrested,* Carol Ann. Tyrus had some pressing business for Tad in Macon. He ran some legal papers up for a court case. Honestly, some folks in Love's Forge can't be happy unless they're spinning fairy tales."

Lady's words come straight out of the honey jar. "Believe me, Carol Ann, if anybody in my family happens to need any prayers, you will be the very *first* person I'll call."

When I come in, Lady puts her hand over the receiver. She juts her chin at one of the soup trays. "Take a tray up to your mother now," she says. "Then come right back down here."

Her up-do has come undone and her silk blouse has a water stain. "All right, darlin'," she sings into the phone. "We appreciate your concern, but truly there's no reason to worry about us. You have a lovely evening."

Lady hangs up the phone, her expression unreadable. I stand still, holding the tray. "Daddy was running law papers up to Macon?" I say. "Before, you said he went to Knoxville."

She is already at the sink, attacking the soup pot with a metal brush. "Yes, Lyndon Baines," she says, banging on pots. "And now he's home. Our family is none of Carol Ann Baggett's business. And that goes for the rest of Love's Forge, Pastor Jinks, the Spurlock clan, and any other nosy parker. Now get that soup up to your ma before it goes cold."

I climb the stairs watching the red soup lap at the edges of the flowered bowl. Concentrating on not spilling. From the landing, I hear Daddy moving around in his bedroom.

I've got my eye on the soup. Step. Slosh. Step. Slosh. I'm creeping past his room when his voice starts up behind the door. The hall is dark. There's the whoosh and gurgle of the toilet flushing upstairs—that must be Grandpa Tad. I hold my breath, take one step toward the door, strain my ears to hear what Daddy is saying. He's muttering, his voice low. Then, "Just one more funeral," he says distinctly.

Did he go to another funeral? Is that where he was all this time? Or somewhere—else? *Disorderly conduct,* Lady said. *Arrested,* Lady said. You don't come home looking like a stray mutt from "running law papers up to Macon."

"Lyndie?" Lady's voice calling from downstairs shocks me into motion. "Get that tray in to your mother and come on down here." It's like she has X-ray vision and can see through floors.

I push open Ma's door without knocking. She has the lights out; she's in bed on her side with the covers bunched up. I balance the tray on her night table and switch on the bedside lamp. "Lady sent up soup."

Ma pulls the sheet over her face. "Leave it, baby," she says under the sheet.

"Lyndie!" Lady barks from the bottom of the stairs.

"Coming!" I tap Ma's thin shoulder under the sheet. "Drink the soup, Ma."

She doesn't move.

"Ma?" I sit down on the bed. Seeing her under the sheet

like this is upsetting. Ma's world keeps contracting smaller and smaller.

How did she go from being a person who wanted to *smash the war machine* to a person who just smashes out kitchen windowpanes?

I shake her shoulder. "Where did you get Daddy from?"

She pulls the sheet closer. "Sweetie pie," she says in a muffled voice. "My head really hurts tonight. Could you go on downstairs now?"

I lay my cheek on her shoulder.

"Ma. Did Daddy, was he—did he do something bad?"

"Lyndie!" Lady's call is pitched one degree higher and one degree louder.

"Maybe we could go stay with your granny and Aunt Pearl for a while," Ma says, muffled into the pillow. "I miss my mama so much."

"But—will Daddy come with us?" I know how she feels. All I want to do is climb in with Ma and spoon against her until our breathing synchs up.

"Ma?"

She doesn't answer me. "Ma, what happened to that gun Daddy had?"

"He pawned it. He says." Ma sighs under the sheet. "Stop fretting, Lyndie."

I shut her door softly on my way out. When I pass Daddy's room my feet slow. The floorboards creak with his pacing, pacing, pacing.

Wednesday. One more day until my oral presentation on D.B.'s narrative, and I'm starting to panic. I'm not used to talking at school, much less in front of the whole class. Plus, everything about D.B.'s life seems so personal and depressing. With Daddy back in the house, I should be able to settle down and pay attention to my homework. But more than ever, I feel like I have angry bees between my ears.

In first-period science class, we have finished our unit on mosses and ferns and are starting on physics. I set up the day's experiment with twitchy Horace Wise, who is my partner. Our experiment involves a ruler and a marble and energy.

Horace sets the marble in the groove of the ruler. "If the ruler is flat, the marble doesn't roll," Horace explains to me patiently, when it becomes clear I am drifting off. "That's potential." He shoves a library book under one side of the ruler. "But lookit what happens when the ruler is tilted."

Horace was born with a problem called Tourette's syndrome. It causes a tic in his face he can't help. It makes him scrunch his nose and yawn when he's excited, which is weird, but also sort of cute. He is also totally enthusiastic about science experiments. I like that about Horace.

"The marble becomes kinetic," he says, scrunching and yawning. We both watch the marble roll along the ruler. "You're supposed to write that down," he adds. *Scrunch. Yawn.* His yawning makes me yawn too, but not so much from being tired as from being anxious.

What if our whole family is actually tilted, like that ruler? How long until his potential energy turns kinetic and Daddy rolls away again? Or worse?

In Time of Test, Family Is Best. That's what the framed needlepoint in Lady's kitchen says. But what if, in times of test, the family is obviously not up to it?

In English, Mrs. Flannigan gives us the whole period to finish planning our presentations with our groups. My team pushes our desks together. "D.B. and I are going downtown this weekend," Dawn says, coolly. I can tell she's making a big effort to talk to me at all. "To distribute cookies to the homeless. Do you want to come this year?"

"I doubt it," I say. "Still grounded."

I want Dawn to argue. I want her to say, *Come on, Lyndie. I have faith in you. You can enter the category of kindhearted people this year.* She doesn't say that, though. She makes a face. "My mom said she would call Lady and ask her if you could come."

"Okay. Well, good luck with that."

PeeWee still has his nose taped up.

D.B. puts on an announcer voice, points at PeeWee. "In *this* corner, Bad-to-the-Bone Bliss. And in *this* corner"—pointing at me—"Left-Hook Hawkins."

"Please. Could we get started," I say, all business.

"Dode worry aboud id," PeeWee says through his taped-up nose. "We will hab a re-batch, ad I will *slaughter* you."

I point my chin at him. "Do you have any idea at all how juvenile it is to put gum in somebody's hair?"

"You broke by dose!"

"Peanut butter will take gum out of hair," Dawn puts in. "Creamy Jif works best."

"Thanks, Dawn. I know that *now*," I say.

Mrs. Flannigan appears at our table. She has her hand on her hip, which is Flannigan code for *suspicious*. "Peanut butter?" she says. "And whose presentation is this part of?"

"We're discussing Dawn's hobbies," I say sweetly. "Her recipe for peanut butter cookies."

"Oh, I see," Mrs. Flannigan says, obviously not seeing.

"For her charity work," I add. "Feeding the homeless."

"And you two." She looks hard at me, then at PeeWee. "I hope you have settled your differences."

Which will never happen.

I sort out all my file cards for my presentation.

Not on the cards: Things I know about D.B. but can't say. Like, D.B. was imprisoned at Pure Visions for lighting an accidental fire. That, according to his dead foster father, he has an invincible purpose stuck to him like a shadow, which has not yet been revealed.

I've got lots of stuff about the name Dalzell. I've got the newspaper clipping about Mac Screaming Eagle Driver. Best of all, I have that extra something D.B. is not going to believe.

The thing I really seem to be missing about his life is a theme. Unless D.B.'s theme is being homeless, which is too dismal to even contemplate seriously.

"D.B.," I say. "Is there something else you can tell me, that you want people to know about you?" I lower my voice. "Apart from the personal stuff? Like, do you see a theme to your life or anything?"

"Yes, a very clear theme: I am never going back to Pure Visions, no way, no how," D.B. says. "Before that happens, I will run away and nobody will ever find me in a hundred and fifty years. I'm going to get out for good."

I imagine D.B. rolling away like a marble down a ruler. "I think what you are talking about is more the *plot* of you than the *theme* of you. Besides, wouldn't running away only get you in more trouble?"

D.B. puts his head on his desk, facing me. "Come down here."

I put my head down too, and our faces are close. It's like we have made our own little private room in the middle of our noisy class. I can smell jujubes on his breath. "Kids die at Pure Visions," he says, breathing cherry-flavored candy. "I'm not ready to die."

Lady has granted me what she called a "special dispensation given the circumstances," *circumstances* being my looming Advanced English presentation, which still has as many gaping holes as one of Dawn's knitted hats. But the special dispensation isn't really about that. What D.B. said about Pure Visions scared the bejesus out of me. I need to find out if what he said, about kids dying there, is actually true.

So, back to the library I go after school. Lady drops me, this time.

I stack Ma's overdue books on the library counter by Mrs. Dooley.

"Back so soon?"

"I need to read up on the history of a place called Pure Visions Reform Academy. See if there's anything in the news."

"I can help with that." Mrs. Dooley says.

Mrs. Dooley helps me look for articles about Pure Visions in the card catalog, then it's back to the microfilm room. I find one article from six months ago about Pure Visions. The story says the school failed an annual inspection, and that the American Civil Liberties Union is filing another lawsuit against them.

"What's the American Civil Liberties Union?" I ask when Mrs. Dooley checks on me.

"The ACLU defends our civil rights, the ones the Constitution says we have, in the Bill of Rights. We all have civil liberties in America that nobody can take away from us. At least," she sighs, "in theory."

"Why would they be filing a lawsuit against a reform school?"

Mrs. Dooley bends to study the article on the lit screen. "Well, go ahead and read down, Lyndie."

The story says it's not the first time Pure Visions has been in legal trouble. Pure Visions has been in violation of state law for excessive punishment practices and for not providing proper medical treatment for the boys.

"You can probably dig up earlier news about it, if you go back year by year," Mrs. Dooley says. "The article is suggesting that the rights of the boys in the school have been violated. They aren't being treated humanely. Even if you're in prison, you still have civil rights. So for example, they can't keep you in dangerous conditions, or anything that causes what they call 'grievous harm.'"

Grievous harm. Putting the *grave* and the *grief* in *harm.* It sounds like serious legal language, language that might translate into "Kids die at Pure Visions," like D.B. said.

"I want to go all the way back to when Pure Visions was founded," I say. "It says here they've been open since 1915. Can you show me how to find articles from the very, very beginning?"

"Young lady, you are a researching machine."

"I like getting to the very truth of what happened. Mrs. Dooley," I say. "I just now decided. I want to be a historian when I grow up."

Grandpa Tad could explain how the ACLU lawsuit works. He'd know if a blood relative to D.B., even if it's a Screaming Eagle relative, could play a part. Would Screaming Eagle have not only shared blood, but shared loyalty to D.B., like Lady's kitchen needlepoint says? A possible plan is taking shape in my mind. It is a plan with parts. I will need help from lots of people, and I will have to confide in them. Many things could go wrong. But if it works . . .

If it works! I feel all light and floaty, thinking about it.

If it works, D.B. will never, ever have to go back to that awful place.

CHAPTER SIXTEEN

It's oral presentation day in Advanced English and I can hardly think, I feel so jittery. When I go outside to feed Velvet and Hoopdee this morning, they are already waiting for me by the front porch, inseparable. Hoopdee has figured out how to unlatch the barn door with his nose and throw his whole weight against it. He's also decided he can take Velvet for a little stroll out any time they have a notion.

Velvet kicks up her heels and runs two speedy circles around the house, showing off. When I peeled away her bandage yesterday, her leg was totally healed. And to prove it, she hops the barbed wire fence into the overgrown vegetable garden and tugs up a mouthful of old carrots that have gone wild. Then she flies back over the wires again and snuffles at the Quaker oats I'm holding in my palm, flicking her ears.

"Steer clear of your father today," Lady says to me when I come into the kitchen. She hands me a platter of scrambled eggs. "Give him some space, you hear me? Let him settle. Don't go stirring him up. Go put these eggs on the sideboard. We're eating in the dining room this morning."

I happen to know Daddy is already stirred up. At one o'clock this morning, he was pacing, talking to himself. And then at four thirty. I woke up both times and listened until it stopped. My worry about Daddy and about my presentation on D.B. got all mixed up in my head and kept me awake too. I realized I had spent a ton of time researching Pure Visions, and that's not even something I can put into my presentation.

At six o'clock, Grandpa Tad knocked on Daddy's door and went in, and I heard them talking. I padded down the hall to Ma's room, hoping to get her to listen to my presentation. I could really use some practice. But she was already in the bathroom and I heard the shower running.

I bring the platter of Lady's overcooked eggs to the dining room, my eyes dry and crusty from lack of sleep. Lady's got polished silver-plate on the table, and cloth napkins and her wedding china. I guess this *is* a special occasion, since every other morning, the grown-ups grab coffee at the kitchen counter, if I see them at all. And here's something I didn't expect: Daddy is limping downstairs. He passes me with a nod and sits at the dining table, awkward and stiff, like he's bruised under his denim shirt and clean khaki trousers. Frankly, he looks terrible. His face is banged up, and his hand trembles when he takes the china pot to pour coffee. He catches me looking and grimaces. But he smells like Aqua Velva, his favorite aftershave.

And, wonder of wonders, Ma comes down too.

I go to the kitchen and Lady hands me a plate loaded with bacon.

"Ma is out of bed," I say.

Lady nods.

"I guess her headache is better?"

"Child, it's not her *head* that aches," Lady says. "Go ahead and take that bacon out now."

I carry the bacon out to the table and slide into the chair next to Ma facing Daddy. Ma pats my hand. The circles under her eyes look deeper than ever. Whatever does Lady mean? If it's not Ma's *head* that aches, what is it?

Lady brings in a bowl of cut-up fruit and a silver rack of toast. I unfold my napkin on my lap and smear my toast with butter, shooting glances from Ma to Daddy, until Grandpa Tad hustles in and plants himself at the head of the table, as if he does that every day. Of the whole lot of us, Grandpa is the only one who looks like he got more than three hours sleep.

"This breakfast is certainly fine, Lady, my darlin'. You fix my eggs exactly like I like 'em," he says.

"We'll eat breakfast together like a civilized family from now on," Lady says.

"Indeed," Grandpa Tad murmurs. "It's nice to have us all here."

Daddy is silent, forking up eggs with a shaking hand.

"Me and Tyrus are going out to the antiques show and auction in Sevierville soon as we eat," Grandpa Tad says.

Ma pushes her overcooked eggs around. She tears a piece of toast into pieces. Why does she *never* eat anything?

Lady's at the sideboard loading up her plate. "I was dearly hoping you and Tyrus would clean out the barn this morning," she says. "There's not a square foot of space left in there."

Daddy can hardly lift his coffee spoon without spilling sugar all over the table, much less haul rusty furniture and farm tools around. Lady must be batty.

"I suppose we can wait until next week, once Lyndie puts that doe back in the woods where it belongs," she adds. "As she promised. Deer do not live in barns."

Velvet. I did promise to let Velvet go on Tuesday. I twist the cloth napkin in my lap up into a ball. "Her leg is still oozy and sore," I say. Not true. But it's worth a try.

Lady puts her plate down and sits. "That creature is covered in ticks," she says, picking toast from the rack Grandpa offers her. "Our whole property will be overrun soon enough; they'll be dropping on our heads from the rafters. And I'll be up a ladder scrubbing the ceilings with vinegar and baking soda till my back gives out."

I jab my knife into the butter dish and carve off a big hunk. Velvet does not have ticks. At least, I don't think so.

Ma dabs her mouth with her linen napkin and folds it neatly by her plate, where she's eaten about two thimblefuls of food. Her shoulders look impossibly thin under her peasant blouse. My parents have not looked at each other once.

Lady cuts her toast in half. "The junk you're storing in that barn, Tad, is a paradise for rats too," she says.

I throw my butter knife down with a clatter. "There are no rats in the barn!" I feel like I could fight every single person at this table with my bare hands until they coughed up some answers.

"Heavens." Lady glances at me. "Somebody got up on the wrong side of the bed this morning."

"And stepped in the pot," Grandpa Tad jokes.

"Vermin are living all over this property," Lady says smoothly. "Which you would know, Lyndie, if you ever cleaned out those traps, like you are supposed to, or followed your schedule, or completed your chores."

"Darlin'," Grandpa Tad says to Lady. "Let's not fuss this mornin'."

"I cleaned out the traps," I say, much too loud. "And it's not my stupid schedule. It's *yours!*"

Daddy startles at the sound of me yelling. He pushes back his chair and half stands, then subsides back into his chair with a pained look on his face.

"Simmer down, darlin'," Grandpa Tad says under his breath. His hand on my arm is soft and liver spotted, and the middle knuckle is swollen; he has the same fine gold hair as Daddy does on his wrists.

"How about this fall weather," Lady says thinly. Totally ignoring me. "This may be the last warm day we get before winter."

We're going to work on helping you control your temper. That's what Pastor Jinks said when I got sent to his office for bashing up PeeWee Bliss. *I had a friend,* the pastor told me, *a Jewish rabbi. Whenever he got angry, he put on a spe-*

cial coat. It took him only long enough to find the coat and put it on to allow his anger to fade away. I want you to think about ways to cool your own anger, Lyndie.

If I don't get a grip on myself, it's going to be Lady ends up with a bloody nose next time, not PeeWee. *Sometimes anger is a feeling we use to cover up other feelings,* Pastor Jinks said. *What feelings might you be covering up, Lyndie?*

When I hop over the Spurlocks' back fence, Dawn is hustling out their front gate. She's curled her hair into ringlets and is wearing pink lip gloss. For the presentation, I guess. Or maybe living with a boy makes you all about hair curlers, who knows? Her knitting needles are out and she's trailing a scarf so long, it's dragging to the ground.

"Hey," I call, jogging up to her. "What's that for? Your pet giraffe?"

"I'm knitting extra-long scarves this year. A needy person could use a scarf for all kinds of things. A pillow, for instance."

"Or he could tie it between two trees and make a hammock," I suggest. "Or use it to escape from a fourth-floor jail window."

Dawn stares at me blankly.

"An angry person," I say, "could wind it around and around their body until they didn't feel angry anymore."

Dawn's needles stop clacking, and she gives me her full attention. It feels like the first time she's really looked at me since school started. "You think that would work?"

"Maybe." I slide my eyes away. Dawn doesn't have the first notion about what's going on in my family, or with me.

And anyway, where would I start? I can already see her shocked face, if I told her how filthy and beat-up Daddy was. That he was maybe in jail, for "disorderly conduct," for a whole week. Her family is so orderly and perfect and happy, with their hot dogs and flop-eared bunnies and lawn games. With their good deeds.

Well, there *is* one good deed Dawn could do for me. "Hey. There's something I need to know about D.B."

"What?"

"What was his foster mother's name, that he had before he got sent to Pure Visions?"

"Um," says Dawn. "Wait a sec. Why do you want that? You're not going to talk about his foster mom today?"

"No," I say. "No, I would never. It's for something else."

Dawn sounds doubtful. "This doesn't seem right. What *something else*?"

"Just trust me."

"I don't want to sound mean, but you don't act that trustworthy, Lyndie." Her voice goes soft, and she blinks

176

down at her scarf, looping green yarn over her knitting needles.

"What? Why?"

"You don't tell me anything anymore. You're all, I don't know, closed up."

"I hardly saw you all summer! Besides, there's nothing to tell."

Dawn shakes her head. "How come you moved in with your grandma and grandpa, then?"

"They're old," I reply. "They needed help."

"That is so absurd," she mutters.

"What?"

"You did not move in to help your grandparents! Do you have *any clue* what a crummy liar you are? And anyway, how can you lie to me, when I'm your friend? It's so wrong!"

"You Spurlocks always know what's the right thing!" I burst out. "How'd you get to know so much about right and wrong? Is that genetic?"

Dawn gathers the long scarf up in her arms and turns to me, her eyes fierce. "You can be sarcastic all you want, but it's not that hard to tell right from wrong. You figure out what effect your action will have on other people. Like, what effect lying to me will have on our friendship. Why don't you think about that."

"But, Dawn . . ."

"But Dawn, but Dawn. Excuses, excuses." I don't think I've ever seen Dawn Spurlock get angry before. She's like a whole different, new and realer person.

"The thing is," I say desperately, "you can never be totally sure of the effect what you do or say will have. If you're *in the middle* of something, you can't see how it all fits together. You never know until after, when you look back. That's the whole point of learning history."

Dawn subsides a little, considering. "Well, maybe." After a minute, she says, "Like homeless Bernadette and the peanut butter cookies."

"Huh?"

"Bernadette, who lives under the bridge, you know, I told you about her. I brought her peanut butter cookies in a napkin. She ate half of one, then shoved the rest up her sleeve. She wanted to save them for later. Anyway, it brought rats. She showed me where a rat came and gnawed on her wrist while she was sleeping. The bite got infected."

"Oh man."

"I felt so bad. You can't always guess every consequence, even if you are trying to do good," Dawn says, a little sadly. "I think, though, you have to, you know . . ."

"You have to try?"

"Yeah," Dawn says. "It's better to try to do the right thing, than not to try." She brushes back her curled bangs. "Now I always take Bernadette her treats in a tin box. Rat-proof. You learn to do better. Like you could learn to be a better friend." Dawn's knitting needles start clicking again, and we walk on. "If I did find out his foster mom's name," she says, "and I'm not saying I will, we would have to let D.B. know. I'm not going to *keep things from him*." She pins me with a meaningful look.

Suddenly, I want to hug her. Only a few months ago, I would have, without thinking about it. And she would have hugged me back. But when I'm about to reach out, she tucks the scarf and her needles away into her book bag and steps away. "I have to hurry to school. I have Math Maniacs study group before first period."

I watch her curls bounce as she trots off. When she gets halfway down the block, she turns and calls out.

"I'll try to get the name, Lyndie."

CHAPTER SEVENTEEN

It looks like Dawn has charmed PeeWee into submission. He's actually arranging photos and poster boards at our grouped desks. His nose bandage has come off. I guess I did no permanent damage.

"Maintain a lively pace." Dawn clicks her stopwatch on and off. "We each have five minutes. That leaves time for audience questions."

Dawn hands me her speech—she's written out the whole thing, and I'm supposed to prompt if she gets stuck or forgets what comes next. D.B.'s role is to scan our audience for signs of boredom. He's supposed to jump in with a joke to liven things up if our audience starts losing focus.

Dawn presents on PeeWee first, so I man the stopwatch. Kids find their desks and D.B. flicks the lights on and off to get everyone quiet. Mrs. Flannigan, with a clipboard, takes a chair off to the side.

In front of the room at the podium, Dawn clears her throat. PeeWee holds up the first photo board, pictures of a barrel-chested young black man. He has a crew cut and a wide-open expression, like he's trying to make sense of the world. "This is Sergeant Demetrius Hallowell Bliss," Dawn says.

"Sergeant Bliss fought bravely in Vietnam. He volunteered early, came home for a short while in 1973, then signed up for a second tour. The official record of his service states that he put his own life at risk many times when his unit was cornered." She goes on to tell about the terrible battle of Fire Base Ripcord that lasted twenty-three days, and how Sergeant Bliss got a Purple Heart medal for his bravery. And how, just a few months before he was due to finally come home for good, PeeWee's dad got killed in sniper fire.

"What does the sergeant's loyalty and courage have to do with PeeWee Bliss, you might ask," Dawn says. PeeWee picks up the second poster board.

Glued on it are pictures of a tiny, thin baby in a hospital crib with a bunch of tubes attached to him, even one stuck in his nose. The baby's face is mushed and bruised as an old apple, and he has on a pale yellow knit cap. Some kind of tape is wrapped around his hands. His skin is so transparent, you can see the veins right through.

"PeeWee shares his father's name, Demetrius," Dawn says, "except his mom and dad called him PeeWee, because when he was born he was only three pounds. Only one percent of babies born so small survive. He was also bleeding inside his head. The doctors said it was unlikely that PeeWee would survive past his first week in this world."

Infant PeeWee is unbelievably cute. For some reason, I think of Velvet.

Dawn nods at PeeWee and he holds up the next board. It is a picture of Mrs. Bliss holding baby PeeWee out in front of the hospital. Her face is so lit up, she looks like she could burst into flames of joy. "But he did," Dawn says. "The nurses in the infant unit told Mrs. Bliss that PeeWee was the strongest little baby they ever met. They said he had true grit. And even though Sergeant Bliss unfortunately did not return from Vietnam because his life was untimely taken, Mrs. Bliss knew that PeeWee had inherited something important from his dad. His name might sound small, but PeeWee has big courage and gumption."

I look from Dawn, to the stopwatch, to PeeWee. PeeWee's eyes are blinking and shiny, but he is also smiling, and his chest is proudly puffed out. I never saw a person looking so complicated.

The class claps when Dawn takes a bow.

"I love the way you made the connection between Pee-Wee's big courage, or what the nurses called *grit,* and his father's, Dawn," Mrs. Flannigan says. "And between Pee-Wee's name and one of his character traits. This is exactly the sort of connection we'll be looking for in the literature we're reading this year."

Dawn blushes to the roots of her curled bangs and hurries back to her desk.

"And PeeWee," Mrs. Flannigan says, "it was very brave of you to allow Dawn to share your story with us."

I'm up next. I hand a rough outline of my presentation to Dawn.

I look out at my classmates and my lips feel dry. Everything I'd planned to say about D.B.'s narrative feels totally jumbled up in my brain with everything I *definitely do not* want to talk about. Fathers, mothers, uncles, ancestors. Arson and straight A's. My folder of clippings trembles in my hand. I have to lean against the podium to get steady.

"You may have noticed we have a new student in our midst this year," I croak out. "Given name, *Dee-Ell* Baily, spelled *D-A-L-Z-E-L-L.* D.B. for short." The class sits silent. "D.B.

has what you would call an illustrious heritage. His strange name comes from the barony of Dalzell in Lanarkshire, Scotland." I fumble in my folder and pull out a map with the county of Lanarkshire penciled in red. "The first recorded instance of this name is from Thomas de Dalzell, who was a war hero at a legendary Scottish battle for independence against the English. The Dee-Ell family even has a coat of arms: sable black with their motto, which is 'I DARE.'

"Here's Fun Fact Number One about D.B. He has heterochromia, which is rare and unusual. That means eyes of different colors. D.B. has one greenish eye and one brown." At this point, I fumble my folder and it drops to the floor, spilling notes.

Dawn is signaling. "Excuse me, Mrs. Flannigan, can I give Lyndie a prompt?" she says.

"Of course," says Mrs. Flannigan.

Dawn hurries over. We scramble to pick up all my papers, and she whispers in my ear.

I stand back up at the podium. "Oh! I forgot to say, D.B. has set himself a personal challenge this year. He is going to live the Dee-Ell motto. He is going to DARE to attempt an astonishing feat, which as far as I know has only been achieved rarely at Covenant. He is going to end his year with nothing but straight A's on his report card. And on top of that . . ."

I stop, confused. Everybody is staring at me. My mind has gone totally blank. I could say, "D.B. eats jujubes for breakfast," and "He's more graceful than he looks," and "He's the most honest person I ever met." But that's not in my presentation. What was I supposed to say next? The class fidgets. My head prickles with panic.

Nobody raises a hand to ask a question. Mrs. Flannigan nods, but she doesn't look particularly impressed with me.

Mrs. Flannigan says, "You've told us a lot of interesting details about D.B.'s family origin, but not much about D.B. so far, Lyndie. Remember, the assignment was to tease out the character traits, the conflict, and the theme of a person's life. Is there anything else you can tell us about D.B. that might help us understand his personal story as a narrative?"

What was important about Thomas de Dalzell, the Scottish hero who fought for independence? I fumble through the papers in my folder again. And then, my brain opens up.

I look out at the class. Their bored faces. "D.B. is a fighter," I say.

Mrs. Flannigan says, "Go on."

"D.B. has an uncle named Mac Screaming Eagle Driver, a champion undefeated welterweight kickboxer." I fish around in my folder and find the newspaper photo, which

I hold up. "This is Screaming Eagle, and he is one tough cookie. The record states that he has TKO'd—that's *technical knockout*—twenty-eight other fighters in a row."

I glance over at D.B., and he is grinning like a maniac. He had no idea I'd found his uncle. He pumps a fist in the air.

Dawn's face is one big question mark. I didn't put this part in my outline.

"Welterweight means you weigh between one forty and one forty-seven pounds," I say. "Oh, and the breaking news is that D.B. is founding Covenant Academy's first ever kickboxing club, open to all weights. I would recommend you sign up quick, because space is limited. It could be a long time before you have a chance to learn from somebody who is the descendent of a famous Scottish war hero, and also closely related on his mother's side to a champion boxer."

Now I have their attention. Most of the boys are leaning forward and watching me. Even the girls have stopped gossiping.

"Furthermore," I say, watching D.B.'s face, "I personally had a phone conversation with Screaming Eagle." D.B.'s green and brown eyes are big as saucers. "Screaming Eagle is maybe a little rough around the edges, as you might expect, but he warmed up quite a bit when I said I knew his nephew. I told him D.B. is starting a kickboxing club. Screaming Eagle said, possibly, if we invite him to Covenant, he might teach a demonstration class. He said he had lost track of his nephew from the time D.B. was a toddler, but that he would be interested to meet him now. Okay," I finish. "I guess that's it."

The class is murmuring. A bunch of kids are wiggling their hands in the air, all excited to ask questions. But Dawn catches my eye and holds up her stopwatch. I've gone over my time limit. It's D.B.'s turn to present. He looks like he's about to burst.

I can't get near D.B. after class. He's surrounded by kids. I catch Dawn in the hall. "Your presentation on PeeWee was fantastic," I tell her. "And D.B.'s talk! I actually learned something about my own family. I never knew Ma met President Johnson."

"He got that from me."

"He did?"

"Your mom told me. She went to the White House with some students from her college to speak to the president against the war."

"Wow. When did she tell you that?"

"One time when I was helping her make waffles last year. You were still sleeping. Remember, you *used to* invite me to spend the night at your house." Dawn takes out a pot of lip gloss and reapplies it to her already shiny lips. "I loved your talk too."

The lip gloss smells like strawberries. Her eyelids have little sparkly flecks on them, like Hillary Baggett's. "I never heard the word *heterochromia* before," she says. "And that uncle! D.B. is signing up lots of kids for kickboxing now. They're lined up in there." She flicks a strawberry-scented thumb at the classroom door. "You did that for him. It was really thoughtful. Doesn't that make you feel good?"

Am I in the category of kindhearted people?

She waves the lip gloss under my nose. "Want some?"

"Since when do you wear makeup? No thanks, Lady wouldn't like it. I'd get a big lecture on proper deportment for eleven-year-olds. She'd probably add on another week of jail time."

"Lyndie," she says patiently. "You would wipe it off before you get home."

"You're telling me to commit sneakery? You, who are such a fussbudget about what's right and what's wrong? What has happened to you? Also, it's goopy. I bet no-see-ums fly into your lips and get stuck."

Dawn puts away the lip gloss. "It's getting too cold for no-see-ums."

"Whoop!" D.B. cries, running down the hall toward us. "Seven kids signed up for kickboxing." He grabs me in a hug, pinning my face to his scratchy sweater, smelling like Woolite. "You are a genius!"

I wriggle out of his grasp. "Seriously?"

"No lie. And, *the most* major thing. You found Screaming Eagle."

We have a twenty-minute break before our next class, so we hurry outside. The air is bright and clean. I'm standing between Dawn and D.B., feeling all over giddy and a little embarrassed from D.B.'s exuberance.

"Screaming Eagle didn't say he would come for sure," I say. "Only maybe."

"It's a start," D.B. says, hopping around. "I'm going to make straight A's and get away from Pure Visions. Maybe my foster mother could have me back. And if not, maybe Screaming Eagle would take me in."

Dawn and I exchange a look. She wrestles a ball of yellow yarn out of her bag. It's attached to a square of knitted wool the size of a potholder. "One stitch at a time," she says, over the clickity-clacking of her knitting needles. "And eventually you have a whole sweater."

Lady has the phone wedged between her shoulder and chin, and her appointment book open on the kitchen table, when I get home from school. "All right, Jessie," she says, "I'll discuss it with Lyndie. We'll let you know."

I throw my schoolbag down on a chair. Lady sets the receiver back in its cradle. "Dawn Spurlock wants you to help distribute cookies downtown this weekend," she says. "Well, you can't fault them for feeding the needy. That was her mother."

I wait.

"Perhaps we could make it a trial run," Lady says.

Is Lady really going to let me join the category of Kids Who Bring Baked Goods to Hungry People in September?

"Do you suppose you've learned anything, from being punished?" Lady asks.

"Are you meaning I'm not grounded anymore?"

Lady gets up and turns her back on me, filling the sink with soapsuds. "I'm considering I might lift your restrictions, partially. Here's what we're going to do. You have permission to go with Dawn and that boy, whatever his name is, the delinquent."

"His name is D.B."

"D.B.," she says tartly. "I suppose that stands for a proper name."

"It stands for Daxx," I say, out of peevishness. "Daxx Bloodboil."

Lady's mouth drops open. "Well, I *never*. You and Dawn and that . . . Daxx . . . can hand out cookies or whatever you have a mind to do, for a few hours on Saturday morning. Then, I want you three to meet me and your mother at the History Museum. I have an eleven fifteen tour to give. We'll take the tour together and have luncheon at a nice restaurant afterward. Your mother doesn't have to go to work until two o'clock on Saturday."

Leave it to Lady to ruin a perfectly fine Saturday of freedom. "Ma won't come," I say. "She'll have a headache."

"There isn't a thing wrong with your mother's head that a day out of that stuffy bedroom and an ounce of gumption won't cure. Lyndie, from now on, we are going to behave like a family. This is your home now."

"So families take museum tours? And have fancy, uh, luncheons?" I know all about family, I used to have a good one, an exactly right-sized family, and we never in our lives had *luncheons* at some snooty restaurant. We had picnics in my tree house. We had road food during trips to visit Civil War battlegrounds. "What about Daddy, then?"

"Grandpa Tad is taking your father to the V.A. hospital Saturday."

"What for?"

"He's due for his annual checkup, is all."

Oh, sure. A checkup. "I want to go with Daddy to the V.A. hospital. I always go. All the veterans know me there."

Lady rinses her hands and turns from the sink. She takes a step over and lowers herself into the chair opposite me, leaning forward on her elbows. "My dear, have you ever heard the expression *choose your battles*?"

I chew my lip and turn my face away.

"For once," Lady says, "you could let go of fighting. You could try to be agreeable."

Which is totally rich, coming from the very Captain and Commander of Disagreeable herself.

CHAPTER EIGHTEEN

On Saturday morning at 8:07 a.m., I wave at Dawn's dad, who's already out in the yard fighting the pull cord on his lawnmower, and knock on Spurlocks' back screen door. I smell pancakes.

"Come on in, Lyndie," Mrs. Spurlock cries.

She's shoveling cookies from wire racks into Tupperware tubs. Pitch and Paulson are making P-shaped pancakes at the gas stove, fighting over who gets to ladle out the next batch of batter.

"My turn!" Paulson squalls. "You already spelled out your entire name!"

"Nuh-uh," Pitch says. "I only did the *P* and the *I* and the *T*."

"Hi, Lyndie," Dawn says. "We made peanut butter chocolate swirl cookies."

D.B. and Dawn are at the kitchen table, vocabulary cards scattered around them.

"And double fudge brownies," D.B. says. "My specialty."

Mrs. Spurlock waves her spatula. "Except he had to eat two entire batches of 'mistakes' before he got a single pan he was happy with."

"I think Mr. Spurlock helped correct a few of those mistakes, to be honest," D.B. says.

Mrs. Spurlock gives me a quick kiss on the top of my head. "What's been keeping you away from us so long?"

I take a seat next to Dawn. Pitch climbs down from his stool at the stove and wobbles over with an L-shaped pancake for me. "Hey, thanks Pitch."

I slather my scrumptious pancake with butter and pour a gallon of syrup on it. I can't remember the last time I had Karo syrup on Spurlock pancakes.

Dawn holds up a flashcard. "Use in a sentence," she says to D.B.

"Abnormal," D.B. says. "It is *abnormal* for a twelve-year-old girl to spend so much time knitting ugly hats."

Dawn smirks and holds up another card. "Dismal," D.B. says. "Knitting is a rather *dismal* hobby for anyone under the age of ninety-seven.

"Dumbfound," he says at the next card. "I am in fact

dumbfounded that even a ninety-seven-year-old could take any serious interest in knitting."

"Pick a new topic please, D.B.," Dawn says.

Next card. "Illiterate," D.B. says. "The exact opposite of me."

"That sentence is illegal," Dawn says. "The opposite of you might be female. Or skinny. Or *melancholy*. Which is also a vocabulary word, by the way."

"Okay. I would be *melancholy* if I was still not able to read good, or stayed *illiterate,* past seventh grade."

"Much better," Dawn says. "Unable to read *well*."

"D.B., you can start carrying cookies out to the car." Mrs. Spurlock points to a mountain of Tupperware. "I need a strong and stable cookie carrier. That description fits you." The sweet-natured tone of Mrs. Spurlock's voice makes me wince. She always talked to me in that kindly way. It felt so genuine.

"Correct," D.B. says. "I am strong, stable, and also *nimble*. I am a *notoriously* good cookie carrier."

Dawn gathers up her vocabulary cards.

"And Dawn," her mom says. "You can get that last batch of cookies out of the oven."

"Really, Dawn." D.B. punches her shoulder, but not hard. "Quit *shirking*. Or you'll *incinerate* those cookies."

"Don't *pummel* me," Dawn responds.

This is what a *home* looks like, if Lady wants a lesson. Alphabet-shaped pancakes, and inside jokes, and little kids at the stove almost setting themselves on fire—

"Hey!" I jump up and pull Paulson's stool back six inches from the gas stove. I turn the dial down low. "Look, this is real hot under that pan. It's open flame and it burns things. Like T-shirts, and the children inside the T-shirts. You have to be really careful, Paulson."

D.B. catches my eye as he's loading Tupperware. "Take it from me, kid," he says. "You definitely do not want to be fooling around with fire."

Mrs. Spurlock drives us into downtown Love's Forge, and we unload cookies into our folding cart. She calls out the car window before she pulls away: "Remember, you're meeting Lady and your mom at eleven fifteen sharp at the History Museum."

"Got it," I call back.

Dawn unfolds her checklist of baked goods recipients and I read aloud over her shoulder. "Lewis Bushyhead. I bet he'll be at the museum today, dressed up like Abe Lincoln. He's not technically homeless or destitute or anything."

"He's in the category of people," Dawn says, "who are

perpetually hungry. Not because they can't get food, but because they feel that the food they do get only makes them hungrier." I love that Dawn remembers our categories.

There are about fifteen people on Dawn's list. I feel like I know them all, because we've talked about them so much over all the time she's been doing Hungry Honeys. The ancient Fry brothers—they lived in the Arcade Motel before it got shut down. Big John Stone, another Vietnam vet. Big John's auntie, who gets hungry between her Meals on Wheels deliveries. Then there's Mrs. Green and her three kids. Her job as a bookkeeper was eliminated. All of them need a lot more help than peanut butter cookies, but Dawn always says it's a start.

"Bernadette under the bridge by Dillard's River," I read next. "Bernadette is truly homeless, and truly hungry."

"Does she seriously live *under a bridge*?" D.B. says.

"No. She's not a wicked troll," Dawn says. "She goes up to the Presbyterian chapel at night, and they give her supper and a bed, with other people who are homeless. She's only under the bridge in daytime. Until it gets too cold, in winter."

"She hates being cooped up," I explain, remembering everything Dawn told me about Bernadette. "She likes to be free."

"We should go see her first," Dawn says.

We head down the sidewalk toward the bridge.

You can see Bernadette's camp from far away. She's made a fort with blankets and cardboard boxes. Unfortunately, we also start to smell her from some ways off.

"Bernadette isn't fond of bathing," Dawn explains. "She's leery of baths because she's got sores, mostly on her feet, and she never had good shoes, so I bring her thick socks. Last Christmas, Pitch and Paulson and I pooled our piggy banks and bought her a pair of super-warm Moon boots."

Bernadette has her Moon-booted feet propped on a box when we walk up. "What do you want? I don't need anything," she says.

"We have cookies and brownies," Dawn says.

"I don't care for brownies," Bernadette says. "Never was a fan of brownies." She's wearing one of Dawn's knitted practice sweaters.

"Okay," D.B. says under his breath. "I am baffled. How could anybody: *Not. Like. Brownies*?"

"She loves brownies," I whisper back. "Dawn says she likes to be independent."

"I don't want any help," Bernadette says, in a high grump. She sounds like Lady.

"We need your opinion on these cookies," I tell Bernadette. "Before we take them to anybody else. To see if they're any good or not. We value your unvarnished opinion."

"Good one." Dawn nudges me.

"Hand them over, then," Bernadette concedes. "But I won't eat food coloring. Did you put in food coloring?"

Dawn opens a Tupperware and takes out the cookie tin she prepared special for Bernadette. "No food coloring," Dawn says. "Peanut butter, chocolate, butter, flour, and lotsa love." Bernadette opens the tin and sniffs.

She bites into a cookie. Chews slowly. "I suppose it's okay," she says.

"Great," Dawn says. "Then we're going to go hand out the rest. Thanks so much for testing them! I'm going to bring you some hats next week. I need to check how they fit before we start giving them away."

"Whatever," Bernadette says.

We haul our pull-cart back up the sidewalk.

"Wow," D.B. says. "That was intense. How long has she been homeless?"

"They told us at the Presbyterian church her brother was Navy," Dawn says. "In Vietnam, his boat sank. She lived with him, but she couldn't keep the apartment after he died. I guess she got depressed. She doesn't have family."

We spend the next couple of hours distributing our

cookies. When we're done, I feel as if each cookie I handed out made me lighter. We have only one Tupperware left, for Lewis Bushyhead, and we have twenty minutes to meet Lady and Ma at the History Museum. We head over to get some pre-fancy-lunch ice cream sandwiches at Pete's Food-Land.

D.B. walks ahead of us and Dawn grabs my arm. "I've got something for you too," she whispers. Pulls out a folded piece of notebook paper and shoves it at me. "Here. Put it away quick."

She got me the foster mother's name.

D.B. turns around.

Dawn widens her eyes at me and points. "Put it away!" I stash the paper into my jeans pocket.

"Remember our deal." She nudges me. "We have to tell him soon."

We park on a bench outside Food-Land to eat our ice cream. D.B. unwraps his sandwich and starts licking the sides.

Dawn hands her half-finished ice cream to D.B. and untangles her knitting. "Your birthday is Saturday," she says to me. "You haven't even brought it up once."

I make a big show of having my mouth full of ice cream, so I can think.

"My mom says twelve is a milestone birthday," Dawn says, clicking her needles. "Remember how much fun we had at my turn-twelve party?"

Six months ago. We baked her cake with help from Pitch and Paulson. We drank root beer floats and stayed up late, watching TV on the Spurlocks' new console TV. So much is different now.

D.B. agrees. "And your birthday doesn't even have to suck as much as my last one. This sounds like a major opportunity for an extra-gigantic chocolate fudge brownie birthday cake."

"Well," I say, swallowing. "Maybe my parents have something planned. I'll find out." I can't hardly invite D.B. and Dawn to Lady and Grandpa Tad's house, not with Daddy like he is.

I look at my watch. "Hey, we need to run, or we'll be late for the museum tour."

I can think about my birthday later. I've got the name of D.B.'s foster mother burning a hole in my pocket, and that's enough to fret about for now.

CHAPTER NINETEEN

When I was seven or eight years old, the Love's Forge History Museum was my favorite place to spend Saturdays. The first thing you see when you walk in the front doors is a sign that says:

THE ONLY THING NEW IN THE WORLD IS
THE HISTORY YOU DON'T KNOW

It was our thirty-third U.S. president, Harry S. Truman, who said that. I think he meant that if you know enough about history, there won't be many surprises, because human nature is human nature. The History Museum was a lot smaller then. Since Lady became chairwoman of the Board of Directors, she raised a lot of money for additions to the building and new exhibits. She also rounded up some people, like Mr. Bushyhead, to hang around in historical period costumes and pretend to be soldiers and Southern belles and so forth.

But back when I was little, it was only three rooms: one for the founding of Love's Forge, one for the Civil War, and one with a big timeline that stretched all the way around, from 1792 to the present, with cases of artifacts that were mostly random stuff people had collected and given to the museum. Around that time I started my own collection of Civil War memorabilia. I thought someday I would make a big donation, maybe the biggest donation of artifacts the museum had ever seen before.

Now, when we come through the front doors, we are greeted by Miss Gregory, who is sometimes a substitute teacher at Covenant, dressed up in a bell-shaped hoop dress with lots of rickrack and poofs that looks authentic, and so does her straw hat. I'm no expert in female fashion of any historical period, but for sure the outfits of the 1860s were dead ugly and smothering, like they were designed to make any Southern female wither like a cafeteria hot dog under a heat lamp.

"Welcome, children." Her Southern drawl is greatly exaggerated.

"Hi, Miss Gregory," I say. "We're taking the eleven fifteen tour with Lady and my ma."

"They're gathering in Room One." Miss Gregory points our way with a folded paper fan. Down the hall, Lewis Bushyhead is coming toward us. He's dressed up in a waistcoat and stovepipe hat. Mr. Bushyhead has become an expert on firearms and infantry tactics since he started working at the museum part-time this year. He can tell you all about how a rifled musket works and why it's no fun to be a Union soldier charging straight at a line of them. His other part-time work is to dress up as a hillbilly at Hillbilly Hideaway Souvenir Store and hang around out front chewing on a straw and scratching under his armpits. He doesn't show quite so much enthusiasm for that job.

"Hey, Mr. Bushyhead," I say. "We brought you cookies."

"Hey, Lyndon Baines. Tell your grandpa, I still got that Foosball table to sell," he says.

Since the Arcade Motel Mr. Bushyhead owned got closed down by the health department, Mr. Bushyhead has had to sell off all the games and toys that made the Arcade Motel a tourist destination. Now he only has those part-time jobs as a phony hillbilly and a make-believe Civil War era man. It was Lady who told me this. She made his story sound like a prediction of my own future, if I don't pull myself together.

Mr. Bushyhead takes the Tupperware Dawn hands him and rattles it, like he's trying to guess how many cookies are inside. He adds, "And tell your grandpa to consider the jukebox too. It don't work, but I can give him a price he can't beat and maybe throw in a snow cone freezer extra."

"A snow cone freezer!" D.B.'s eyes are wide. "How cool is that?"

Lady pokes her head out of Room One. "Lyndie, bring your friends in here. We're about to start our tour."

There are ten other people waiting for the tour, out-of-town touristy types with a couple of sullen teenagers in tow, plus Ma, who is looking about as spritely as I've seen her in a long time. She's got her hair pulled back and she's wearing a skirt and sweater set that has to be some of Lady's doing.

Ma pulls me close and gives me a kiss on the top of the head. She wraps Dawn in her free arm and kisses her too. "Ma, Lady, this here is D.B.," I say.

"Well, that was a lovely introduction," Lady huffs. "My stars, what do I have to do to teach this child some manners."

"Oh, pardon *me*. May I introduce you to D.B.," I say in a prissy voice. "D.B., please let me present my grandmother Mrs. Hawkins, and my mother, also Mrs. Hawkins."

"It is an honor to meet you, Mrs. Hawkins the First and

Mrs. Hawkins the Second," says D.B., with a little bow. The bow is sort of charming.

"The pleasure is all mine, Daxx," Lady says, not showing evidence of any pleasure.

D.B. raises his eyebrows at me when Lady turns her back. "Daxx?" he says.

"It's your Criminal Mastermind name," I say. "Daxx Bloodboil."

D.B. aims a bark of laughter into his collar. His face is pink with joy. "Oh," he gasps. "I totally love that."

"We'll get started now," Lady says. She marches forward, *tick tick tick,* on her alligator pumps. "This way please."

The first room is dedicated to the founding of Love's Forge. I know the contents of this room by heart.

"Love's Forge was settled by Mordecai Alexander in 1810," Lady tells us. "In 1817, his son-in-law James Love built an iron forge on the west fork of the river. Love's forge played an integral role in producing metals for farm implements and building materials. You can still see the site of the old forge today," she says. "Generations of Love's Forge citizens have made it a beloved family tradition to visit there."

D.B. and I exchange an eye-roll.

"Excuse me, Lady," I pipe up. "But Love's Forge was not

settled in 1810. There were people here for fifty thousand years before Mordecai Alexander."

D.B. elbows me in the ribs. "Good one," he says under his breath. The tour group murmurs a little.

Lady, who I know was about to launch into a speech about the Old Grist Mill, stops cold. For a second, she seems flustered. Then, when I guess she's going to snap hard at me, she draws a long breath.

"Thank you, Lyndie," she says evenly. "Ladies and gentlemen, this is my granddaughter Lyndie Hawkins. She's quite the historian. Lyndie, why don't you tell us what you mean by that."

I feel heat rush to my face. Now I'm in it. "Well," I croak out. "What this place was, before James Love and his father-in-law got here, was called the Indian Gap Trail." I hesitate.

Lady says, "How fascinating. Please continue."

"This whole area was inhabited by many different native tribes from prehistoric times, and was later settled by Cherokee—not that they would have thought about it that way. The problem was, the Cherokee signed a treaty that turned the whole big land that they lived on over to the state. This was in about 1785. The treaty allowed white people to settle here for the first time."

I'm a little out of breath and my heart is pounding. But the tour people are all looking at me, interested. "Did the Cherokees get something? In exchange?" a teenaged boy asks, seeming slightly less sullen.

"The history books say 'clothes and other goods.' After the treaty, white people flooded into this whole area, hundreds and hundreds and thousands. Mordecai Alexander was one of them," I say.

I glance over at Lady. I can't tell if she is furious or proud of me, because she sort of looks like both.

"So were my own Hawkins ancestors," I add.

"Thank you for that important footnote, Lyndie," she says. "Now, let's move on into our Civil War exhibit."

"What you said about the Cherokee treaty that opened up their land to white people—that's not exactly what I'd call a *footnote*," D.B. says to me as we're walking down Main Street to the fancy restaurant lunch. Or, one of us is walking. D.B. is prancing and spinning, practicing *axe kicks* and *cut kicks*.

"No one talks about that treaty here," I say. "Same as people don't talk about the Civil War being fought over enslaved people."

There are certain pieces of history you learn not to talk about, or even think about, when you live in Love's Forge.

"History is written by the winners," I say, remembering the quote from Winston Churchill, though he used the word *victors*. Mr. Handy wrote that on the chalkboard.

D.B. spins to face me. "I know it," he says. I shove my hand in my pocket and wrap my fingers around the note Dawn passed me. I'm hoping Pure Visions is not going to turn out to be the victor when D.B.'s history gets written.

At the restaurant, we eat our "luncheon," as Lady calls it. I order turtle soup with a splash of sherry in it, which tastes very dark and a little chewy, and Dawn has an omelet with real truffles. Ma orders a Waldorf salad, and actually eats the bulk of it, for a change. Lady nibbles on mushroom toasts. And D.B. wolfs down a hamburger with French fries.

Lady keeps calling him *Daxx,* which makes D.B. squinch his face as if he is in terrible pain, but in fact is meant to stop himself from dissolving into fits of hysterics. As soon as he can gasp out a sentence, he starts asking Lady a million and one questions about the Hawkins Homestead. How did they build the log cabins? Where did the wood come from? Who taught them how to do it? Did they have help?

"Fayette Hawkins and his brother Trevaill carried each

one of those white oak logs from the forest themselves,"
Lady says. "And they carried every stone for the foundation." There is a soft light in her eyes. "I'll bet you didn't
know, Lyndie, that my own daddy Waldrop and I used to
visit the Hawkins place when I was a child. That was when
I first laid eyes on your grandfather; we must have been
eleven or twelve years old. About your age. He was a little
scamp, Tad was. Oh, how he used to make me laugh."

I didn't know that. I don't think I ever once imagined
Lady could have been a girl like me. Or somebody who
could laugh at a boy's jokes.

"Thank you for lunch, Mrs. Hawkins," D.B. says sincerely.
"Those were the most scrumptious French fries I ever ate."

"Well, you're quite welcome, Daxx," Lady says with
as much warmth in her voice as I've ever heard. "Maybe
next time, you'll broaden your palate and try the *Duck a
l'Orange.*"

After lunch, Lady goes back to do another museum tour.
Ma takes my face between her palms to kiss me good-bye.
"You stood up for what's right," she says, arching an eyebrow. "The tourists on that museum walk learned some real
history today." She climbs into the Blue Bullet and rolls

down the window. "You're an inspiration, Lyndie B.," she says before she drives off to work.

D.B. and Dawn and I pool together the few bucks we have in our pockets to buy Bernadette a winter coat, which Dawn will give to Bernadette to "try on, to test whether it is warm or not," on her next visit. Now we are waiting for Mrs. Spurlock to pick us up outside Nate's Nearly New Thrift Store. D.B. and I dissolve into peals of giggles recounting our luncheon.

"Duck a l'Orange!" D.B. says. "What the heck is that even?"

"If you had bothered to *broaden your palate,* Daxx," I say in Lady's high tone, "you might know the answer to that question."

"You're lucky you have grandparents to tell you about your people," D.B. says. "Your grandma is okay."

Secretly, I'm the tiniest bit irritated that Lady and D.B. seemed to have hit it off.

"She's not going to be making you any sugar and butter sandwiches," I say, a little huffily. "You can bet on that. But I'm sure she'd be thrilled to make you a schedule, if you ask her nicely."

CHAPTER TWENTY

The second I get home, I run upstairs to my bedroom and dig into my jeans pocket to read the note Dawn passed me.

I sit on my bed and unfold the paper.

I can't believe what I'm seeing.

It's the name and address of D.B.'s foster mother. But the impossible part is, there can't be many people with that name, in that town. I stare at the paper, my memory swirling, and replay everything I know.

What does this mean? What are the chances D.B. would have *this* foster mother? I sit in shock for three, four, five minutes. Daddy is still at the V.A. hospital with Grandpa Tad. Suddenly, I wish I could ask him a ton of questions.

That woman has had sorrow piled on top of sorrow. To have her husband do such a terrible thing. It's more trouble than anybody deserves.

I fold the paper and put it in my bedside table drawer. Dawn made me promise I wouldn't keep this secret from D.B. too long. But the name on that piece of paper makes everything lots more difficult.

On Monday morning on my way in to school, I pass D.B.'s new kickboxing club. A bunch of kids have gathered on the quad in the bright, clear air, a couple even from the upper grades, and D.B. is there, sliding a tape into a portable tape deck. PeeWee Bliss is already busting moves. He and Jarrod Pierce and Frank Stoppard and Drew Spurlock, Dawn's tenth-grade cousin, are messing around, trading fake philosophy from the *Kung Fu* TV show:

"*Never assume that because a boy has only one pimple, he cannot squeeze,*" Drew intones in a solemn voice.

PeeWee raises a finger and rolls his eyes heavenward. "*When you can flush the toilet as fast as a cobra striking, your poo will not stink up the school,*" he says.

The boys fall all over themselves laughing and shoving and throwing clumsy kicks at each other. Looks like D.B. is no longer in the category of lonesome kickboxers. Did my presentation really have something to do with that, like Dawn said? I wonder if I am helping D.B. find his invincible purpose.

"Okay everybody," D.B. calls. "Listen up. Today's objective is to get your muscles warm, and I'll show you a little bit of technique. Right now, you can jump or dance or move however you want."

D.B. presses the play button on his tape deck.

The music picks up steam. D.B. catches my eye and beckons to me. "Come on, Lyndie! Set yourself free!"

I shake my head. I'm not going to be jumping around with all those horrible boys.

D.B. runs over and grabs my hand, insistent. "Come *on!*"

Reluctantly, I let him drag me into the quad. At first, I move like my feet have two separate minds. I sort of hop around, arms flailing.

The boys are totally cutting up. Nobody is paying me any mind at all. After a minute I start to feel myself falling into the groove.

D.B. bobbles around with me, laughing hysterically. And then he executes some of the most beautiful kick-air punch-spin sequences. It's unbelievable. I mean, D.B. is heavy. How does he make himself fly?

"Okay, guys," D.B. yells. "Hold up and I'll show you a couple of simple stances."

D.B. demonstrates: side stance, front stance, back stance. He tells us about cultivating fire in the belly: "A vigor and a passion," he says, "but it's something that *you* drive. It doesn't drive you. There's a big difference. *You control the fire.*"

By the time we have done stances for ten minutes my legs are aquiver. But I'm taking control of my fire.

D.B. is so happy, he's practically wriggling. "Now. Get fierce, warriors!" he calls. "I want to feel your fire!"

A bunch of kids have stopped at the quad on their way into Covenant. Even Hillary Baggett and Sara Jane have paused to gawk at us. And there's Dawn.

I'm feeling a different kind of fierce, full of complicated gratitude. I run over to Dawn. "Dawn." I'm still breathless from kicking and spinning. "Thank you, thank you. For getting the name. You are a true friend. I promise I'll be a better one."

Once school lets out, I run home to spend my last day with Velvet. I promised to let her go tomorrow, a promise Lady has not let me forget for two seconds. I find Grandpa Tad on his knees in the barn, trying to crack open an old footlocker with a screwdriver. Hoopdee and Velvet are nearby, Hoopdee watching Grandpa closely like he's trying to learn a new trick. Grandpa Tad pushes back his hat when I come in. He squints at me against the light in the barn door.

Grandpa Tad has been pawing away at his junk pile in the barn as long as I've known him, but I can't hardly tell any difference. A mess of rusted lawn chairs looks like it's in the "To Go" section, but otherwise, he's shifting random items from here to there. It hurts Grandpa Tad's heart to have to let loose of so much as a burnt-out lightbulb. He has a soft spot for unworkable things.

Grandpa gives the screwdriver one more whack and the lock springs with a clatter. The lid creaks when he opens it. "Empty! I was darn sure I'd find a trove of Roman coins."

"Hey, Grandpa Tad." I move into the dim clutter. Velvet hops over to me and I toss my arm over her neck. "Mr. Bushyhead said he's got a Foosball table to sell," I say. "If you buy the table and his busted jukebox, he'd throw in a snow cone freezer extra."

"Your grandmother will have my head if I put one more antique anything in this barn," he says.

"You should switch to small collectibles," I say, "like me. They take up lots less room." Velvet dances around me. She doesn't like being cooped up. She wants to go out for a run.

Grandpa Tad shifts an armload of rubber hoses three feet. He straightens his back with a wince.

"Hey, Grandpa?"

"What is it, sugar?"

"You know the boy at Spurlocks', D.B., how he is from that juvenile center in Knoxville, Pure Visions?"

"I did understand that."

"Would there be any way, any lawful way, to get him released back to his foster mom? Even if he committed arson?"

"It's a shame that boy ever got tangled up in the legal system. But now he's in it, I guess that would depend. Does he have any living family?"

"Yes," I say. "There's an uncle. A kickboxer named Screaming Eagle. He lives in North Carolina."

"Maybe if the uncle and the foster mother petitioned the court. Or maybe somebody could work with Child Protective Services. He must have had a social worker at some point. Could be quite a bit of luck, to get all those pieces to fit together."

"Pure Visions is bad."

"I know it. That place has been in and out of the news long as I remember, always on the verge of getting shut down. There's been rumors for years; folks say it's not normal, the number of boys who die there."

"I read the ACLU has a lawsuit against them."

"You don't say."

Velvet butts me with her head. She's getting really antsy.

"Do you think we could try, Grandpa?"

"I have a lawyer friend argues cases for the ACLU." Grandpa Tad's jaw is working while he's thinking this over. "It'd be a challenge. Is he a good boy?"

"He's the best."

"I'll tell you what," Grandpa Tad says. "I'll look into what we might could do for your friend. We'll try to find his foster mother."

I think about how joyful D.B. looked out there on the quad doing his kickboxing. Once I set this ball rolling, there's a big chance it will upset Daddy. I remember the poem he told me about—the one about the soldier who went home only to find a big dark hole. Daddy crying while we drove around in the car so late at night.

But D.B. deserves to be free.

Velvet butts me again, harder, and kicks up her heels. Insisting: *Let's go out!*

"Bigwitch," I say. "His foster mother's name was Janet Bigwitch. She lives in Cherokee, North Carolina."

When I go out the next morning to feed Velvet and Hoopdee, I stroke her ears and try to pretend today will be the same as any other day. I have pondered every which way I might turn her loose. I could walk her deep into the woods and leave her with a bowl of oats. I could ask Grandpa Tad to drive her somewhere safe. Velvet is so bright and full of vigor. She should not spend her life cooped up in a barn.

Hoopdee pushes his whole body against my legs, like he knows it's time.

At our "family breakfast" in the dining room, nobody says word one about Velvet, but I know we all know it's today. And though I've asked four times since Saturday, once to Ma, once to Daddy, once to Lady, and once to Grandpa Tad, none of them has told me the first thing about how Daddy's checkup went at the V.A. The silences that swallow up the important stuff that happens in this house make me feel like I'm walking around in the Land of Holes.

Of all the real things we could talk about, our whole conversation around the table goes like this:

Lady: "Lyndie, a spoon is not a shovel. Please take smaller bites."

Grandpa Tad (rattling his newspaper): "Well, will you look at this. They've got pictures of the *Titanic* sunk at the bottom of the Atlantic now. Somebody sent a submarine camera down there."

Daddy: "Pass the salt, please."

Lady: "The salt and pepper shakers travel around the table together, Lyndie, not separately. They are a married couple."

Ma (mutters): "Oh, is that how it works?"

Ma does have a touch more color in her cheeks. Daddy's eyes are still bloodshot, but what little smile he has for me reaches a bit farther into them. When I'm clearing our plates, he sees the army ring on my thumb. He twitches his eyebrow at me. Then holds my thumb for a few seconds. "You are welcome to that ring. The only reason I have to be glad I went to war is you."

"There could have been easier ways to get a daughter, Daddy."

"Yes, but . . . Not any daughter would do. I wanted a stubborn, sassy know-it-all, one brave enough, or foolhardy enough, to be my copilot."

Hope rushes through me. He is definitely better. But I'm scared, because I don't know how to help D.B. without conjuring back Trilby.

All day at school, I keep that fire of hope in my belly. If things are getting normal in this house, maybe I could even invite D.B. and Dawn up here for my birthday.

At 2:45 on the dot, I'm banging through the screen door of Lady and Tad's house, thinking how sweet Dawn and D.B. were when I told them about having to let Velvet go. They handed me tissue after tissue until I hardly felt sad anymore, just loved.

I find Lady in the parlor on her knees sorting through fabric swatches and rags from her old quilting trunk.

She doesn't even look up at me. "Jessie Spurlock called this afternoon. Dawn is asking about your birthday now." Lady tugs an old jacket of Grandpa Tad's out of the trunk. "Glory be, if I never got another phone call from Jessie Spurlock I'd think I died and woke up in heaven. I told Jessie we were planning a small party for you here, with only family this year."

I bite the inside of my cheek.

She pulls out a silk dressing gown, a moldy dress shirt, a pair of ancient jodhpurs. "Where is that old overcoat of your grandpa's? Your mother has finally taken my advice to do something with that weedy garden. Now she has a mind to make a scarecrow. Life is too short to lie in bed. She's been stewing in her own juice long enough."

Looks like Lady is well on her way to putting Ma on a schedule too.

"I had to make Jessie understand, this is a special occasion, my granddaughter turning twelve. You need your family close around you."

"Lady," I say. "I'd like to invite Dawn and D.B. to come up. For my birthday."

"We'll bake a strawberry shortcake, like your mother and I used to do, when you were little. It was your favorite. You remember your strawberry shortcake?"

I do. I *didn't* remember it was Lady and Ma who made the cake together. I have a flash of a memory: me and Ma and Daddy and Lady and Grandpa Tad around the kitchen table in our cottage. Lady looking still young, Ma in her strappy summer dress. The warm wind stirring the lace curtains and the smell of cut grass and candle wax and strawberries all mingled together.

"I want to invite D.B. and Dawn," I say, one notch louder.

"Oh, good grief, child."

Lady takes an armload of folded plaid fabric from the trunk and spreads it out on her knees. "I bought this plaid to sew your school uniforms, when you were starting into third grade at Covenant," she says, smiling. "We were so *proud* to see you in that uniform. That was back when I had a lot of time on my hands."

"Lady!" I stamp my foot hard on the parquet floor.

222

She startles. But she says calmly, "Don't you shout at me, my girl."

"I want to invite them. Two friends. For my birthday."

"Lyndie," Lady says, struggling to her feet and smoothing her skirt. "We're going to have a nice birthday here, a quiet birthday. With your daddy and mother and grandpa. Like a family." What the heck is she smiling like that for?

Sudden rage boils up through my belly and into my throat, coursing down my arms. "I had a family! A father, a mother, and me! The mother did not have headaches. The father did not disappear for days! We had picnics and road trips! We read books together! We invited my friends for birthdays! I want to go home to my real house!"

"Hush! Hush now." Lady drops the jacket she's holding and moves for me.

"I don't want this family!"

Lady comes for me, grabs my shoulders. She's going to slap me hard, I know it. But she doesn't slap me. Instead, she pulls me into a smothering hug. "Oh," she says. "Oh, Lyndie."

The parlor door opens and Grandpa Tad steps in. "What's all this?"

Lady's unclamps me, and I fall away from her. Grandpa Tad puts a hand on top of my head to keep me from pushing past him. "Well now," he says. "Well now." I twist under his hand. When I look up at Lady, she is pink-faced, her hand covering her mouth. Grandpa Tad stands there in silence, for once without a word to say. He turns me loose. "Go on, then," he says quietly.

Gladly. I bust out of the parlor, slamming the door behind me.

By four o'clock, I've cried until my throat feels swollen. Grandpa Tad comes to the barn and finds me and Velvet and Hoopdee curled up in a heap.

"Sugar," he says, squatting down next to me.

"Why is she so mean?" I ask him.

"Your grandma wants what's best for you. Wants it so bad, it hammers her heart."

I squint through my tears at Grandpa Tad.

"What about what's best for Velvet?" I sob. "She's got nowhere to go."

"I'll take her in the truck myself and drop her somewhere she'll be able to make a nice home for herself, all right? She's plenty big enough to survive on her own. She looks to be about four months old." He gives Velvet a pat. "Look, you've healed her leg up so nice. You did her a very good turn, Lyndie. She was lucky you found her. You gave her a chance at life she wouldn't have had otherwise."

I gave her a chance at life.

Grandpa Tad gets to his feet. "Come on now, you can help me load her into the truck and say good-bye proper. Your Velvet is going to live her days out now according to the purpose she was meant to fulfill. That's the best any of us can hope for."

Velvet follows me up the ramp into Grandpa Tad's flatbed, docile as you please. I encourage her to lie on the blanket Grandpa put there. I give her a quick kiss on her warm nose and climb down.

Hoopdee keeps jumping into the flatbed. I pull him off, he hops up. I pull him off, up he gets again. Finally, I have to leash him. "You took good care of her, Hoopdee," I say through my sniffling. "She was never meant to stay with us permanent. She needs to be free."

We watch Velvet's head poking up over the back of the pickup, her nose in the air and her ears flicking with excitement, until Grandpa Tad's truck turns out past the gate and around the curve of the high ridge road.

CHAPTER TWENTY-ONE

The next day, I don't speak one word to Lady. We sit at our fancy breakfast, eating to the sound of clinking silverware on china, and Lady blathers about the weather, or bosses everybody to do this or that. She barely seems to notice my silence. After breakfast, instead of going back to bed like usual, Ma goes out into her garden to put up her scarecrow. And for the first time in months and months, Daddy has on a dress shirt and pressed pants. He sits at the dining table after I clear it, circling newspaper ads for Help Wanted.

If Daddy goes out looking for work, he could get a job. There will be no more shooting guns off porches. No more disappearing for days and days. He could make enough money for us to buy our home back from Wally Grubecker, and we could be who we were again. No daily schedules.

TV shows after supper. An upstairs phone with privacy. And best of all, no Lady Hawkins. Behind my back, I clasp my own pinky fingers together and shake on it.

By Thursday and Friday, my fury over my lonely, friendless birthday party has turned into a dull ache. I answer Lady's questions about my homework or chores in monosyllables.

Grandpa Tad has no news for me yet about the ACLU lawsuit against Pure Visions.

Even with my small flare of hope about Daddy maybe finding a new job, I would gladly spend all day in my room with my nose in a book, having a headache.

By the time my birthday arrives Saturday, my mood has lifted one notch. I can manage short phrases when Lady asks me a question. I spend my whole birthday outside with Hoopdee, wandering up and down the mountain. I keep an eye peeled for Velvet, wondering if I'll ever see her again, even though I know Grandpa Tad took her a long way off. There's a scent of early snow in the air. I spot coyote tracks. I know it's coyote because the claws are not retracted like a bobcat's would be—you can see the toenails in the print. Daddy taught me every fact I know about animal tracks of any sort. I really loved the dad he used to be.

When I go into the house, Lady and Ma are in the parlor

hanging a string of letters that spells out *Happy Birthday 12-Year-Old Lyndie Hawkins*. I manage a half smile.

At 4:30, both Grandpa Tad's truck and Daddy's Blue Bullet are gone from the driveway. "They had errands," Lady tells me, putting her macaroni casserole in the oven. "Why don't you go put on one of those beautiful dresses hanging in your closet, Lyndie?"

"It's only family, why should I get all gussied up? Anyway, I outgrew those dresses."

"And never wore them once. I'm going upstairs to have a bath and I'm putting on something nice, even if you won't."

I help Ma mix up the batter for strawberry shortcake, like we used to do back home. I'm standing over the bowl of the mixer waiting for the butter and sugar to achieve "fluffy."

"Don't keep starting and stopping that mixer now, let it alone," Ma says. "Your cake won't rise if you keep changing the speed. The butter will separate." Ma took the day off from work for my birthday, special.

When I've finally gotten to "fluffy," she sifts the flour over the bowl and folds it in with a spatula. She sticks her finger in for a taste. "Yummy." Ma has been strangely cheerful for days.

"I guess we should have been feeding you cake batter all this time," I say. "To fatten you up."

"If I could eat cake batter every day of my life, I would."

The doorbell chimes. Nobody ever rings this doorbell. I raise my eyebrows at Ma. She points with the spatula and I go see.

There's a strange couple at the door. The female has huge waves in her hair, and she's wearing kitten heels with a black velvet and gold-skirted dress that has a sash at the waist. The male has on a silk shirt designed with peacock feathers, and a pair of sunglasses propped on his head. They are holding boxes wrapped in glittery paper with curlicue bows.

"You have the wrong house," I tell them. "The Hollywood celebrity party is down the road."

"That party got cancelled," D.B. says. "We thought we'd crash this one."

"Even though we *weren't invited*," Dawn says slyly.

Behind me, Lady is coming downstairs. I smell her My Sin perfume before she puts a hand on my shoulder.

"Dawn, you know you are always welcome in this house," Lady says.

Wait, didn't she specifically tell Mrs. Spurlock *no party*?

"As are you, Daxx." She looks D.B. up and down in his silk peacocks. "That's quite an adventurous shirt you have on. I suppose now you're here, you may as well stay. We'll be having supper soon."

They all smirk at each other. Lady takes their wrapped gifts and goes to put them in the parlor.

We head into the kitchen. "What are you *doing* here?" I whisper to Dawn.

"Lady called my mom and invited us," she whispers back. "We were supposed to go visit my cousins this weekend, but Lady asked Mom as a special favor, to let us come. She wanted to surprise you."

Okay. That's totally weird.

Lady comes in and sits straight in her straight-backed chair. "Look how pretty Dawn is," she says. "I fail to see why Lyndie can't occasionally get herself into a dress."

"D.B., come help with this whipped cream," Ma says. Which he is happy to do. He stands with the whipped cream nozzle on high alert, waiting for Ma to finish sorting the strawberries.

Lady says, "Lyndie, pull my casserole out of the oven, please. And use the thick oven mitt, no *not* that kitchen towel—you'll sear the hide right off you."

I set the macaroni casserole on a trivet. Macaroni casserole is my favorite.

Lady tilts up to look out the window at our empty driveway for the third time. "Where are those men?" she says. I look too, for the third time.

"Dawn," Lady says, drumming her fingers, "are you going to dancing class on Fridays?"

"Yes, ma'am," Dawn replies.

"Does Hillary Baggett go? And Sara Jane Hart?"

"Yes, ma'am," says Dawn. "They do."

"You see what the nice girls in your grade do, Lyndie. The girls from good families."

"It's tough to get to dancing class when you are *grounded*," I remind her. "And Hillary Baggett may be a *nice girl*. But she is not a nice person."

"Her mother, Carol Ann, was a Tri Delt with me at Vanderbilt. I believe Hillary will do fine for herself in life."

"She says mean things about our family," I say.

Lady raises an eyebrow. "Well. The Hart girl, I hear, won first place at a harp recital in Sevierville. Meanwhile, that viola Grandpa Tad brought you last Christmas is gathering dust, I imagine."

"Daddy told me my viola practice sounded like somebody plucking a live mallard duck one tail-feather at a time," I tell Lady. "He said I can't carry a tune in a bucket with a lid on it."

D.B., losing patience with Ma and her strawberries, is pretending to decorate the entire countertop and all its contents with whipped cream. He fake-squirts over the soap dish, the faucet, the cookie jar, then up his own arm and over his shoulder and into his mouth again, where he gives himself a real dose.

Lady's hands freeze on the tabletop. "Listen to me, my girl," she says. "Tonight you are twelve years old. Time to migrate your manners into something this family can be proud of. Dawn, I'd appreciate your good influence. What a fine little miss you have turned out to be."

"Did your grandma make you play viola and dance fox trot," I say, "when you were my age? Because regular modern children in 1985 do not do these things anywhere outside of ass-backward Love's Forge."

D.B. chokes on a mouthful of whipped cream.

"*What* did you say?" Lady clamps her teeth together and draws herself up. She's going to dress me down good for saying *ass-backward*. Maybe wash my mouth with Ivory soap—she actually did do that once, when I was nine and told her something was *damn straight*. I scuttle back in my chair to give her some space.

But I see how disappointed she is, that I would say such a thing aloud, and in front of company. A little niggling caterpillar of shame gnaws at my heart.

I've almost made up my mind to tell Lady I'm sorry. But a commotion of gravel out in the driveway stops me.

Instead of chewing me out, Lady pops up to look through the kitchen window. Grandpa Tad's truck is pulling up, with the Blue Bullet coming in behind it. Hoopdee jumps out of the flatbed.

Lady starts fussing with the flowers on the table, patting at her up-do, muttering about *men,* trying to cover over how relieved she is to see them get home.

Something in me lets go of a worry too. Daddy is safe and sound. He can go out, and he will come back. The screen door screeches open and bangs shut. Hoopdee runs in, skittering into the kitchen, pulling the cold, leaf-smelling outdoor air with him.

"Get that hound out of my house," Lady says to no one in particular.

Nobody moves to get the hound out.

Ma hands the spatula to D.B., and he licks all the strawberry jam off it in a very thorough way. "Lyndie," Ma says, "take your cake to the dining room."

I skate across the kitchen and vault over Hoopdee, who has thrown himself down in the middle of the rug like he's perfectly at home.

"Nice work with the whipped cream," I tell D.B. I offer him a "High Five, Down Low," then fake him out with a "Too Slow," leaving his hand slapping empty air.

"Oh. You did not. Do that."

Before I can get around D.B. with my cake, here they come. Daddy and Grandpa Tad, stomping their feet and harrumphing. The two of them have brought something into the hall, big as a table, covered up with a sheet. Daddy catches my eye and winks at me.

"Lord have mercy, what have they got this time?" Lady says. "Those men are going to have a heart attack. Or surely give me one."

"Something under a sheet," I say, pulling my head back into the kitchen and setting the cake back down on the counter.

Grandpa Tad is pink-faced when he pops his bristly head through the kitchen door. His horn-rim glasses fog up from the warm kitchen. "No peeking, Lyndie. Today is your lucky day," he says.

"Is that my present?" I jump up on a chair and stand on my toes to see over Daddy at the sheet-covered thing in the hallway. "What is it?"

"Oh my stars," Lady says. "Now our young monkey is standing on chairs. What next, the flying trapeze?"

Ma comes over wiping her hands on a tea towel. Lady glances up at her. "Well, Rainbow, you're raising a daughter who stands on chairs."

"Maybe she has to stand up high to rise above all your sniping and carping, Lady," Ma says briskly.

Daddy inserts his hulk between me and Grandpa Tad. He's in a high mood, his whole self seems relaxed and easy.

"Evening, all," he says. "I woke up with the strangest feeling this mornin'. Something special going on. But I can't for the life of me think what. Anybody help me out?"

"You are the proud owner of a twelve-year-old trash-mouth," Lady mutters, back on my case again. "And good luck with that."

"Where is she, then?" Daddy squints at me. "Couldn't be this squirt here, she's way too scrawny for twelve. And the other one, over there"—he points at D.B.—"has got a mustache starting. So I'm hoping that can't be my daughter."

Daddy's teasing makes happy shivers run down my spine. Daddy nods at Dawn. "Hey to you too, stranger. Look at you, all grown up."

"Nice to meet you, sir." D.B. starts to hold out his hand to shake, then changes his mind. He's all sticky with strawberry jam.

Daddy eyes D.B. up and down in his silk peacocks. "Wearing an earring. You in one of those boy bands or somethin', Jewelry?"

"No band yet," D.B. says. "I'm waiting on Lyndie to

take up her fiddle." He grabs Dawn and swings her once around. "I'm thinking, a square dance band."

"Right, whatever happened to that *fiddle*?" says Grandpa Tad. "One of my better yard sale finds."

"Wherever it is, I hope it stays someplace good and quiet," Daddy says. "Not that Lyndie wouldn't be brilliant at anything she put her mind to." He waltzes over, wrapping me in his arms. "Happy birthday, darlin'."

His breath smells like whiskey straight out of the bottle.

CHAPTER TWENTY-TWO

While D.B. and I are arguing over how to set the dining table, whether the fork goes left or right of the plate (*Left side*, Dawn referees), and where to put the milk tumblers, and Grandpa Tad's and Lady's tea glasses (*Right over the knife*), at the same time I've got one ear cocked, listening to Daddy in the kitchen, trying to make sense of him. He's joking and talking a mile a minute, like a kid who got home from riding the Holy Rollercoaster all day at ScriptureLand.

Dawn makes all the cloth napkins into little swans, one for each plate.

"Where'd you learn to do swans?" The things Dawn knows how to do always surprise me.

"Home ec club, last year," she says. "You really should join at least one club, Lyndie. It's good for making friends."

"Hard to join a club when you're grounded every minute," I mutter.

"Maybe. But you didn't join last year either."

The grown-ups roll in carrying macaroni casserole, green salad, and yeast rolls. We settle in and Lady barks, "Napkin, Lyndie." Daddy says the same jokey prayer he always says—

Dear Lord,
Oh bless this food before us set,
it needs all the help that it can get.

Which sends Lady's frozen smile into sub-zero, and then Daddy says, raising his water glass, "To my darlin' daughter." He seems all right. Maybe he only had a tiny sip of whiskey?

Lady and Tad murmur and lift their tea glasses. Ma takes a drink of water. We kids clink milk glasses.

"If you were Scottish, Lyndie," D.B. says, "we'd give you a slippery nose. My grandma used to do that on my birthday."

"Huh?"

"Grease your nose with butter to make the bad luck slip off you."

"Charming," Lady says.

Daddy slings an arm around Ma's hip while she's circling the table dishing out the macaroni. "Rainbow my love, you look too fine for this humble Southern table tonight." For the compliment, Ma adds another scoop of macaroni to his plate. She lets his arm stay where it is for a few seconds before she moves on.

"Hey, Jewelry?" Daddy says to D.B. "Who gave you that haircut? Only time I ever saw a cut like that was on my grandmother's prize purebred poodle."

D.B. forks up a hunk of macaroni that could halt a Mack truck. "Miss Smitty did it down at the school office."

"She copied it off a design from *Dog Fancy* magazine," I joke.

Daddy guffaws and tilts back in his chair.

"I guess Lyndie hasn't gotten you up to speed yet, Jewelry," Daddy says, "but our young men in Love's Forge generally avoid dressing like that, what's-her-name, Madonna? Let's hope Herk Spurlock can sort you out right quick. Keep you in one piece."

After supper, we traipse into the parlor, all but Daddy. I hear him bang out the screen door. When I look through the parlor window, he's got the door of the Blue Bullet open. He's bent inside, so I can't see his head. At first I think he's getting me another present. But his head stays in there too long, and when he comes back in to the parlor, he's empty-handed.

Lady parades in the strawberry shortcake, and everybody starts singing "Happy Birthday." I huff out all the twelve candles plus the one for good luck with a single breath. Ma cuts the cake and passes slices around on the Hawkinses' best china dessert plates.

The cake is one thing that never changes. It tastes exactly the same, clouds of whipped cream you could sink your whole face in, half-sour strawberries mingled with buttery pound cake, and last of all, that sliver of earth-and-honey strawberry jam. In other words, perfect.

Ma's birthday present for me is a signed first edition of *Storm Over the Land: A Profile of the Civil War,* by Carl Sandburg.

Grandpa Tad hands me an envelope with two twenty-dollar bills in it. From him and Lady.

"I hope you will put that toward one decent dress," Lady says.

Dawn's gift is nestled inside tissue paper. It's the gargantuan green scarf she's been knitting for forever. "Your pet giraffe won't miss this?" I tease. The scarf must be six feet long. It has white snowflake patterns knitted into the green. They are cool colors. Soothing colors. Maybe, like

Pastor Jinks told me, I can use this scarf for anger management. By the time I wrap this extra-long scarf around me, the snowflakes will have tamped down my hot mood. And whatever other feeling the hot mood is supposedly covering up. "Thank you, Dawn. I needed this." No matter what we say or don't say, Dawn knows me.

I tear open the shiny wrapping paper on D.B.'s gift. It's a book called *Introduction to Asian Martial Arts*. The cover shows a samurai galloping full tilt on a horse. The horse looks like it is snorting blood, and its rolling eyes are like the eyes of a wolf. The warrior has a sword clutched in his fist.

"Is this so I can practice being a samurai warrior at home, until Lady eases up my schedule so I can join your kickboxing club?" I cut my eyes at Lady.

She shakes her head like she's exasperated. "Young ladies from good Southern families do not take up kickboxing," she mutters.

D.B. grins. "Look inside."

I turn to the cover page, and there's an inscription. *For Dalzell, the best "son" a "dad" could ever wish for.—Trilby Bigwitch.*

And underneath that, *Dear Lyndie, here's hoping you learn to do something less dangerous with that vicious left hook you've got.—D.B.*

"My foster dad gave me that," D.B. says. "Take good care of it."

"Wow," I say. "Wow, D.B., are you sure?"

"Presents you give somebody should pinch a little," D.B. says. "That's how you know they mean something."

"Oh my," I say. "I will surely treasure it." But I close the book up quick lest Daddy get a look at that inscription.

Daddy's present is a Civil War bullet collection in a matted display case: a percussion cap from North Georgia, a pistol ball and a .69 caliber round ball from Shiloh, and a .50 caliber three-ring bullet from middle Tennessee. I think it's the best present ever. But when I look at Ma her expression is frozen, her lips compressed.

Lady gets up abruptly with a lot of noise and fuss and collects a few plates, piling them up on top of one another and banging silverware. "Come on, Rainbow," she says. "Let's wash up."

I put the bullet display case on the floor and cover it up with wrapping paper.

"And," Grandpa Tad announces. "Are you ready for it?" He stands up and swipes the bedsheet off the huge present they carried in. It's Mr. Bushyhead's Foosball table.

"No way!" cries D.B. "I can't believe you are so lucky! This is too radical."

Daddy and D.B. and Grandpa Tad drag the Foosball table into the center of the parlor. I look around the room, and I swear it hardly feels like the same house. All during my party, Lady has been stepping over Hoopdee on the rug like she's never had a rule against inside dogs. The silk cushions on the sofa and love seat are askew. And there's a Foosball table front and center! Plus, they are already banging away at it, spinning the poles like pros.

Dawn squeals when D.B. kicks his first ball into Daddy's goal. Hoopdee lopes around the table, *Yo!*-ing when anybody scores.

Daddy and D.B.'s Foosball game ramps up. It keeps getting wilder. D.B. scores three goals against Daddy, and Daddy uses some language Lady would not approve of. They finish their first game, with Daddy losing 6–2, and Daddy bangs out the front door again. His boots drum down the porch steps. Then, minutes later, back up. The screen door slaps behind him. I'm cutting myself another piece of strawberry cake when he takes his place again at the Foosball table.

"Don't think you can wiggle out of a rematch, Jewelry," he says. On their second game, D.B. starts to wince at how intense Daddy is. He's really banging away on that table; the noise reverberates in my bones. But D.B. holds his own. He shrugs and calls to me, "Your dad plays fierce."

Dawn bounces by the table, clapping when D.B. scores, but she keeps catching my eye. Dawn doesn't care for strong language. I can tell Daddy has unsettled her. And he has unsettled me too. I don't like his grin, which is not a real grin. Or the heaviness of his boots when he moves. Neither does Hoopdee, who has left off cheerleading and come to lean against my legs.

And then, after Daddy and D.B finish their second game and stop for a break, Daddy picks up my birthday samurai book and leafs it open.

I jump up. "Daddy!" I cry. "No!"

But it's too late.

"Trilby Bigwitch," Daddy reads the inscription.

Grandpa Tad throws me a curious look. "Tyrus, you were in Battery A with a fellow called Bigwitch, am I right? Your buddy that passed, a few weeks ago?"

D.B. stops chewing, his mouth full of cake. "What?" He swallows hard, looking at Daddy. "You knew Trilby?"

Any drop of cheerfulness he has left drains from Daddy's face. "Yeah," he says. "I knew Trilby. How did you know him?"

"He was my foster dad," D.B. says.

Daddy studies D.B. Slowly, a recognition dawns. *"You* were the boy? The one who lit Trilby's house on fire?"

For a minute, D.B. looks completely crushed. He seems

to crumple in on himself like a balled-up rag. But then he steadies and takes a breath. He sets his unfinished piece of cake back on the plate. "It was an accident." He looks ready to burst into tears.

"You," Daddy says. "Here in my own house. What are the chances?"

"Son," Grandpa Tad says, watching Daddy's face. "Let's not hash this business out tonight. It's your daughter's birthday." Daddy ignores him. Hoopdee shudders on my feet.

"Lyndie, what is going on?" Dawn has sidled up next to me. I feel her arm pressed against mine. "What is this about?"

D.B. slinks away from the Foosball table toward me. I don't want to blink.

"It's nothing, Dawn," I manage.

"We need to go," D.B. whispers near my ear.

Daddy sits down hard and fumbles around in the inside pocket of his jacket. "No, it's *something*." He pulls out a flask. "Something that calls for a toast." There's so much sadness in his voice. "To Trilby, the best man I ever met. Who saved my life." He uncorks the flask. Takes a long swig, and another, breathing sour apples. "What do you say, Jewelry? You want to drink a toast with me? To commemorate the man whose house you burned down?"

Dawn's hand flies to her mouth.

D.B. wheezes out a horrified breath.

Grandpa Tad leaps to his feet right as Lady hustles in and starts picking up wrapping paper, gathering the last of our cake plates. Seeing our stricken looks, she stops short. Her eyes follow the silver flask Daddy is holding as he lifts it to his lips. In a few seconds, she seems to register what is happening. "Tyrus," she says carefully. "Son, why don't you put that away now. Go on up to bed."

"Excuse me, Mother," Daddy says, "but I am a thirty-seven-year-old man. And I am not ready to go to bed."

"I think you are." Lady's hand hovers in the air, as if she could levitate that flask full of whiskey across the room.

"I don't believe anybody tells a man what to do in his own house. Oh," he says. "I forgot. This is not my own house."

"Tyrus," Lady says. One word. His name, no more. But I can hear all the words underneath it.

"You don't like it, Mother, you are welcome to go to bed yourself."

"Tad." Lady pivots to Grandpa.

Daddy stands up and leans against the Foosball table. "You know—" Daddy crosses his arms. "You'll have to take me as I am. You're the one wanted me moved back in here."

"Of course I wanted you home." Lady clutches the cake

plates she's holding. "What mother wouldn't want to help out her son? But not so that . . ." She lets the words trail off. "You know I don't want liquor in this house."

Grandpa Tad steps forward to reach for Daddy's flask. "Boy, listen to your mama."

Daddy makes a clumsy move to stop him. "Wanted me home *so much*," he says to Lady. "Pushed and nagged. Nudged and nosed. You should have left us alone. You can't fix the unfixable." He takes another swig. "Got to finish the game. I can win this thing."

Daddy's focused on D.B. now, his shaggy red head swaying like the head of an angry bull. "Let's go, Jewelry."

"That's enough, Tyrus. Go to bed," Lady says. "You've had too much and that's enough."

D.B. has got Dawn's arm; he's pulling her toward the parlor door. He's moving so carefully, like if he puts a foot wrong Daddy will charge him.

But Daddy wouldn't hurt D.B. Wouldn't hurt anybody. Would he?

D.B. chokes out, "I have to go now."

"No, you don't have to." Daddy puts down his flask and moves for D.B. "Not before we finish this game."

D.B. backs up quick and Daddy lunges awkwardly after him. He grabs ahold of D.B. by the collar of his peacock-blue shirt, and shakes him like a puppy. "Come on, Jewelry.

Let's you and me go outside and have a private talk about finishing what we start."

D.B.'s face is white. "Let go."

Before any of us can move, Daddy's dragged D.B. into the hall.

Dawn cries, "This is wrong! Lyndie?" But I'm stuck in place. "I'm calling the police." Dawn turns and sprints for the phone in the kitchen.

D.B. is windmilling his arms, hitting nothing but air as Daddy pulls him out the door and down the front steps. Lady runs from the kitchen. "Tyrus, let that boy alone!" Grandpa Tad thumps down the porch stairs. And then Ma is dashing past me out the door and into the yard. In all the confusion, D.B. manages to shake himself loose from Daddy's grip.

And as soon as he's free, he whirls and runs. Fast, his feet kicking up grass behind him. I watch him disappear downhill, a flash of peacock silk. A silver hoop in the moonlight.

Daddy spins and pushes past Grandpa Tad, past the three of us on the porch gaping. His boots thunder upstairs. His bedroom door slams.

Dawn is crying. "I've got to go!" she sobs.

"Wait, Dawn," I plead. "It's too dark now."

"I know the way," she calls, already running past Ma in the yard. "I have to."

Uphill along the high ridge road come the flashing blue lights of police cars. The lights turn at the gate and make swirling blue patterns on the gravel as the cruiser pulls up. It's that same policewoman and her partner climbing out, the ones who were here when Daddy and I got home twenty-four hours late from Trilby's funeral.

"Not one word, Lyndon Baines," Lady says under her breath. "Your daddy has been through enough. He won't go to jail tonight. Get that dog quiet right now."

I snap my fingers at Hoopdee and he slinks up the steps. Sits on my feet, panting and shivery with nerves. Ma comes up too and waits next to us, breathing hard.

"Ryan Todd," Lady says evenly as the pair of police walk up.

"Mrs. Hawkins. We got a call about a disturbance?" The policeman flips open his notebook. "A girl, Dawn Spurlock, called. What's the problem?"

I move from behind Lady, and he fixes on me. "Where's your pa now?"

"Surely you have some real crime to solve, Ryan," Lady says. "Keeping the world safe."

"Things are a bit slow in the 'real crime' department in Love's Forge, Mrs. Hawkins. The girl who called said Tyrus was banging somebody around. A young man, staying with the Spurlock family."

"That boy comes from a juvenile facility in Knoxville," Lady says. Her face is fixed, her eyes like flints. "He's a nasty little piece of work. I told Lyndie she ought not to have him up here."

Lies.

"Where's Mr. Hawkins now?" the policewoman says. She's studying my face, concerned.

Lady says, "He's gone to bed early. As I'd like to do too. Now, Officer Todd and Officer . . ."

"Salazar," she says.

"Officer Salazar. You know my son is a veteran. Tyrus fought proud and hard to keep us all free. The least we can do is give him a night of uninterrupted sleep."

"We are all very grateful for your son's service, Mrs. Hawkins." Officer Todd does not look particularly grateful. "Anybody want to tell me what happened?"

Nobody does. He glances at Ma. She is mute as a piece of wood.

He turns to me. "Did you see what happened?"

I hesitate, then nod.

"Go ahead and tell me then, young lady." He fidgets with his notebook, glances over his shoulder. Like he can't wait to get off our porch and go home.

My grandmother puts a heavy hand on my shoulder. *Loyalty makes you family.*

I keep my voice even. "Daddy didn't touch D.B. Daddy wouldn't hurt a kid, ever. D.B. got mad because Daddy beat him at Foosball. And then Daddy teased him pretty bad about it. D.B. lost his temper. Pushed the Foosball table over."

"Is this your statement?" He looks at Lady, doubtful. Ma's mouth is pursed into a thin line.

"It certainly is our statement," Lady snaps. "My son served his country with great courage and dignity. He is sleeping. That's all you need to know."

Officer Ryan Todd sighs. "With all due respect, Mrs. Hawkins. This won't be the first time Tyrus has been in trouble lately." He glances at me and lowers his voice. "We had him in a cell downtown for three days, you remember. Begging your pardon."

Lady's jaw sets. "On your way out—" She crosses her arms, lifts her chin. "I hope you'll recall the many brave men who sacrificed their lives for us. I hope you'll salute the U.S. flag at our gate."

"You might want to replace that flag," Officer Todd says.

"It's pretty tore up." He snaps his notebook shut. Officer Salazar, the policewoman, hands Lady her card before she walks to the car. "If you think of anything else you want to tell me," she says, "please call me."

"I surely will do that." Lady drops Officer Salazar's card on the porch table like it's a hot potato.

"Everything is fine," I say loudly, for no good reason. The police get back in their car.

I turn and bolt upstairs with Hoopdee on my heels, slamming and locking my bedroom door.

Ma knocks softly while I'm huddling with the sheet over my head. She calls my name once or twice, rattles the knob. Hoopdee whines, but I don't answer. Her footsteps pad down the hall to her own room.

Dawn called the police on us.

Lady says what we do is nobody's business. Nosy-bodies cause more pain and heartache than I will ever know, she said.

When you're in the middle of it, how do you know what's the good side to fight for? What happens when you have to choose between your father and your friend?

Later, I wake up with a gasp, streaming with sweat, from a dream of D.B. being roughed up by prison guards. He's crying, pleading. *Please, please.* It's 3:15 by my watch. And it's not D.B, but Hoopdee, who is whining like crazy. He keeps leaping up at the window, over and over, trying to see over the sill. I haul myself up, stiff and shaky, wanting air. "What is it, Hoops?" I push open the casement window and draw deep lungsful of cold. Hoopdee plants his paws on the sill and looks with me.

Out there in the garden, there's movement.

Someone is walking; the plants are shivering and rustling. Daddy.

He's got something gripped in his fist.

I move from the window, open my bedroom door slow. "Stay here," I order Hoopdee. One slow step at a time, praying the floorboards don't groan to give me away, or that Hoopdee won't start up barking, I creep downstairs.

Last spring, before I knew for sure Daddy had lost his job, I came across him talking to nobody in our living room.

I leaned against his shoulder, snugged my arm inside his, holding on. His eyes turned away from whatever story he was telling himself and focused on me. It was the first time he talked to me about Vietnam in our whole life together.

He told me a story how, a long time ago in the Vietnam villages, the people developed their own art of fighting, a kind of boxing called Vo Binh Dinh. They were light and fast and slick against the clumsy European invaders.

He said that day: "Much as I hated those North Vietnamese, Lyndie, there was part of me understood why they wanted to fight us. They'd been invaded over and over. They wanted their own country back. To finally be free.

"Right and wrong is always complicated," he said. "But then after a while, over there, it felt wrong, with no right involved at all. We couldn't predict what effect that war would have, on Vietnam, and also on America, you understand? We couldn't see, while we were in the middle of it. But your ma always knew that war was a dead end.

"There are so many sides to the story." His eyes were searching into mine. "But I did come home in one piece. And I went to play pool that night, and met your ma. And now I have you. That's the rightest thing I know."

So many sides to the story.

Now I go quiet out the kitchen door, opening it slow. Daddy is walking toward Ma's new scarecrow. Slowly, slowly, I slink toward the barbed wire fence that surrounds the garden.

His back is turned to me, and he stops short when he comes up on Ma's scarecrow. Daddy's shaggy red curls blow in the cold wind. He stands there staring into that scarecrow's awful mirrored eyes. The moonlight glints on the thing he's holding. It's the gun. The gun he said he pawned.

I've got my hand wrapped so tight on the wire fence, it's only when I open my fist I realize I've poked a barb into my hand. Blood is smeared on my palm.

Daddy is talking to the scarecrow—serious and intense, like he is confessing or negotiating or offering the straw man some kind of ultimatum.

Oh please, oh please. Make him calm down. Make him stop.

Then, sudden with one motion, Daddy raises his gun— and fires. The head on Ma's ugly scarecrow explodes in a shower of straw and bits of cloth and red yarn. The sound of gunfire echoes up and down the mountainside. Daddy lowers the gun a foot and shoots again. Aiming right at where the straw man's useless, straw-man heart would be.

Then Daddy turns the gun and points it at his own, living heart.

CHAPTER TWENTY-THREE

No!" I'd cried out. Daddy startled and spun round. And Grandpa Tad and Lady and Ma banged out the door and came running.

They took Daddy to the V.A. hospital that night.

One week and two days ago.

Today, in civics class, Mr. Handy writes a sentence on the board. "If you only learn one thing in my class," he says, "I hope it's this one."

Those who cannot remember the past are
condemned to repeat it. —George Santayana

"It's not only about what we actually forget, but also the history we deliberately suppress, or distort, or lie to ourselves about. Take thirty seconds and think about it," he says.

We all go quiet.

"Can anybody give me an example of a piece of history that we seem to have deliberately distorted?"

Nobody offers an answer. Mr. Handy catches my eye. Raises one eyebrow. "Lyndie?" he says gently.

Something in me wells up. I haven't said three words in this class in nearly a whole month of school. "I guess," I say, "it happens all the time."

"Go on," says Mr. Handy.

"Like, the Cherokee Indians were marched practically right across our backyards when they had to walk on the Trail of Tears to Oklahoma." My voice is shaking.

The class rustles. They're mostly doodling with their heads down. Or staring out the window. Or passing each other notes. Nobody will look at me. Everybody in this whole school knows what happened at Lady and Tad's house the night of my birthday.

They know D.B. ran away and was lost for two days.

They know the police finally caught him hitchhiking toward Raleigh, North Carolina, probably to look for his uncle Screaming Eagle.

They know Daddy got taken to the hospital.

They know D.B. got shipped back to Pure Visions.

But I'm the only one who knows this: *Kids die at Pure Visions.*

"That's a perfect example," Mr. Handy says. "The forced evacuation of the Cherokee people was one of the great tragedies and injustices of American history. And it happened right here under our feet. The way to truly honor that injustice is to remember it honestly, and to learn from it."

That's what D.B. said to me, first time we met outside Pastor Jinks's office. He said if he was honest about setting fire to his house, he might not have to go back to Pure Visions. *I need to be* perfect *this year. I can't get in trouble,* he said.

Mr. Handy turns to pull down the movie screen.

"Today we're going to learn about a person you might not have heard very much of." The slide projector beams up a photo of an old lady in a rocking chair. She's a mass of wrinkles, wearing a white shawl and granny glasses. "This is Sojourner Truth," he says. "She's as important to our modern understanding of the Civil War as any general or president. She was one of our great African American civil rights activists."

Mr. Handy flips through the slides. He tells us about how Sojourner was enslaved in New York, sold with a flock of sheep, but she escaped. She dropped her slave name and called herself Sojourner Truth, and she devoted her entire life to abolishing slavery, and to equality for all women, and to human rights for everybody. Sojourner Truth lived a very long life and even protested to stop segregation on streetcars, all the way back in 1865.

Things were so hard for Sojourner. But she didn't stop trying.

After the slide show, we all file out for lunch period. I go sit on a bench outside to eat my sandwich alone. Even Dawn won't speak to me now. There's no point in going to the cafeteria. She'll be sitting with PeeWee and Sara Jane, or maybe even Hillary. They won't invite me to put my tray down at their table.

Sojourner Truth makes me think of Ma protesting the war. What made Ma stop her activism, and what made Sojourner keep on? How do people get the courage to stand up, and *speak truth to power,* like Ma used to do, and keep on speaking it? Will I ever have that courage?

If I hadn't woke up from my nightmare and looked out the window, Daddy could be gone forever, like Trilby Bigwitch.

I tear the crusts off my peanut-buttered bread and feed them to the sparrows hopping around my ankles. *Sojourner* means "traveler," we found out. She called herself *a traveler to the truth.*

I think the truth is a place you can only move toward, like walking toward the horizon. Even though you know you'll never get all the way there.

CHAPTER TWENTY-FOUR

This week, nobody cares if I do or don't follow my schedule. Ma and Lady are in and out of the house, their voices low behind the parlor door. Lady hasn't exactly said I'm un-grounded, but nothing stops me dragging my feet or taking detours while I'm walking home from school. I perk my ears for a crunch of leaves in the woods. Where is Velvet now?

Hoopdee follows me as he pleases, nobody saying "Shoo!" He sleeps on the throw rug by my bed. With Daddy in the V.A. hospital, Lady's too distracted and distraught to complain about any *houndy odor*.

Only way I can keep moving is to follow my schedule. My schedule doesn't feel like a prison now, it feels like a plan. I empty the mousetraps. I water the ferns. Set out my notebooks on the claw-foot desk. I unpack the last of my boxes. Some pieces from my Civil War memorabilia, the ones I want to keep, I arrange in the bookcase: the locket with the pictures of husband and wife. The Carl Sandburg biography Ma gave me for my birthday. The folding telescope and the domino set made of bone. But not the Civil War bullet collection in a matted display case from Daddy. It will have to go to the History Museum. I can't stand the thought of bullets around me now, but it will make part of a fine exhibit on the Civil War.

I sort my library books: *To Read, Already Read, Overdue But Want to Read Again.*

Today, I'm home from school for a half hour when Grandpa Tad pokes his head into my bedroom. "Sugar, I'm leaving to visit your dad at the V.A. I bet he'd be glad to see you. Want to join me?"

Over this week, Grandpa Tad asked me to go to the veterans' hospital three times. Lady and Ma made the hour drive each way to see Daddy every day. So far, I've always said no.

But learning about Sojourner Truth in civics class, it knocked something loose in me. I think I know what I need to begin to do. Sojourner said, "Truth is powerful, and it prevails."

One stitch at a time, like Dawn says. *And soon you have a whole sweater.*

"Hold on," I tell Grandpa Tad. The birthday box with Dawn's knitted green scarf is on my bed. I unfold it from the tissue paper and wrap it round and round me. Grandpa Tad watches, head tilted to one side, eyebrows raised. "Looks like you're ready for the storm of the century," he says.

"Okay, Grandpa," I say. "I'm ready to go with you."

The hospital smells like iodine and bleach. But Daddy's room isn't too awful—a metal bed, two chairs, a color TV on a stand, *Newsweek* magazines on the night table. He's sitting in a chair by a bright window, his lunch tray on his lap. A football game is on, turned low. He cuts into a chicken cutlet with a plastic knife. There's a green salad too, half a loaf of fresh bread, and a plastic dish that looks like it once was pudding, with the foil peeled back, empty.

He looks up and smiles at me when we come in, and the smile reaches all the way up into his eyes.

I let myself down into a chair, not too close to him. The room is warm, but I pull my green scarf close, imagining knitted snowflakes cooling me, and glance at Daddy through my eyelashes.

His hand shakes a bit, cutting into the chicken. He catches me staring. "The doctor is giving me something for this," he says. "It's . . ." He puts down his fork, holds his two trembling hands up. Frowns. "It's, well Lyndie, the truth is, my hands shake like this when I don't drink. Don't drink liquor, that is. It will pass."

Hearing him say "don't drink liquor," it opens a small space in me for something real to take up room. I knew he was drinking whiskey. I knew it couldn't be good for him. I pull my scarf tighter and try to fight down the lump in my throat.

Most of our heroes have flaws and complications, Mrs. Dooley told me.

"Lyndie."

That little empty dish on his tray. He ate the pudding first, before his chicken. He used to go through our pantry at home. Sneaking down at night to eat the Hostess pies. The Tootsie Rolls. The Lucky Charms.

"Lyndie," Daddy says.

Only a month ago, we were at Trilby's funeral. I picture Daddy the night of my birthday, and I have to take short shallow breaths because the room starts to go white and floaty.

Grandpa Tad says, "They're going to be moving your

daddy over into the psychiatric wing. Day after tomorrow. He'll be there for a bit, then come home." His voice sounds loud, close to my ear.

A psychiatric wing?

"When I do come home," Daddy says, "I'll be going to counseling three days a week. Sometimes, you and your ma might come with me."

I struggle hard to pull myself together, gripping the seat of the chair. I focus my eyes on the floor. Finally I win the battle against the lump in my throat. "Lady will have a fit," I say. "She'll never let you go to counseling."

Daddy clears his throat. "I think she will," he says. "Either way, this isn't about Lady. Lyndie," he says gently. I still can't bring myself to look at him. "Do you want to ask me any questions?"

I shake my head.

"All right." He forks up some salad. "You minding your grandma while I'm gone?"

I sit silent, pulling my chin down inside the scarf. The scarf is scratchy and smells like Dawn's Caswell Massey rose soap.

"You and your grandma are like two pit bulldogs in a bag," Daddy says. "Always have been, from the first time she held you, and you puked up on her new dress." He puts his tray aside. "Maybe you two could try to cut each other a little slack, someday."

He offers me his pinky to shake on it. But this time, I don't shake back. After a minute, his hand drops and he takes up his fork again.

I thought loyalty meant sticking up for Ma and Daddy. Meant putting up my fists every time anybody called Daddy "coward," or "traitor," or "crazy." Meant lying to the police to protect my father. But now, I believe loyalty is lots more complicated than that.

I think about loyalty on Wednesday, when we are given a writing prompt to: "Write about a classmate you admire. And why."

I think about loyalty in science class, where we are learning about forces, like magnetism and gravitation, and why things attract or repel each other.

And I think about it in civics class too, because we are discussing citizenship and "mutual obligations," which is loyalty between citizens and government.

When I get home from school, I go into the kitchen, unwrapping my green knitted scarf, and pick up the phone, thinking about that classmate I admire, and why.

Of course, I still know Dawn's phone number by heart.

"Hi Mrs. Spurlock," I say when she answers. "It's Lyndie. Is Dawn there by any chance?"

Mrs. Spurlock is quiet for a minute. "Lyndie," she sighs. "I think maybe you and Dawn should take a break for a while."

"Please," I say. "I have to ask her one thing."

"She's doing homework. Can Dawn call you back?"

"I really need to talk to her now. I promise it will only take a minute, Mrs. Spurlock."

"Are you all right, Lyndie? Is your ma and Lady and Tad okay?" Her voice is wavery with concern. "I called, but your grandma has been so busy." Yes, Lady has been. And this time, Mrs. Spurlock hasn't come running up the hill with her famous shoofly pie.

"We're all right," I answer. Then: "No," I correct myself. "We're not okay. Not really."

Mrs. Spurlock's silence carries all the words I know she wants to say. "Just a minute." I hear her calling Dawn's name. Then muffled talking; she's got her hand over the receiver. After a while, Dawn comes on.

"Hello."

"I know you don't want to talk to me."

"Mom doesn't want me on the phone."

"I know. But." Something breaks in my chest. "Can I

come down there?" Behind Dawn, I hear Pitch and Paulson arguing over something.

"No, sorry, you can't. I have to go."

"Dawn," I cry out. "I need help. Please."

When Dawn shows up at our driveway gate, she has on a knitting reject Christmas sweater. One arm is longer, so she has it rolled up.

Dawn is quiet while we're walking downtown. It's hard to know where I should start to try to be loyal to her now, with all the secrets I've kept from her. How can I explain my family? Or how I've been caught in the middle of it so long, I can't clearly see the links in the history chain?

"Dawn," I begin. "You know me about better than anybody. But there's lots you don't know."

I start by telling her about the whiskey bottle I found in Daddy's glove box, and what we saw and did on that road trip to Trilby Bigwitch's funeral. And then I tell her everything else.

The Love's Forge police station is on the corner of Main and Mason Streets, in the center of town.

When we haul open the glass doors and walk into the

lobby, I wonder: How will the link I'm adding to my history chain connect to something in my future? I stand still, not able to put one foot forward or one foot back.

Dawn sees me hesitating. "You said you were going to do this." Her face softens when I still can't budge. "It's better to try to do the right thing, than not to try," she says. "Remember?" She gives me a push forward.

A young officer at the counter is doing something efficient with a stack of carbon copies. Dawn flops down in a plastic chair, rolls up her long sleeve again, and drags her knitting out of her purse. She catches my eye over her ball of yarn and tilts her chin at the front desk. "Do it," she mouths.

"Could I talk to Officer Salazar?" I ask Mr. Efficiency.

"Name?" he barks.

"Lyndie B. Hawkins."

"We're busy." He indicates the carbon copies.

"Would you mind checking?"

He gives me an icy look. But he walks off, grumbling.

I slump next to Dawn in a plastic chair. Her needles *click, click*. We're the only people in the place.

The officer comes back and waves me through. I follow his perfectly straight shoulders down into a long hallway of offices. "In there." He points to an open door.

"Officer Salazar?" I poke my head in.

"Oh. Hello. Miss Hawkins. Come sit down. Push the papers off that chair. Put them on the floor there. There's plenty more where those came from."

I sit gingerly and take a breath. It's so hard to know how to start. "Can I try on your hat?" I point at the police cap set on another stack of papers.

"Sure." She hands it over and I put it on. "Hey." She nods approval. "That looks nice. Maybe you have a future career in law enforcement."

I point to my chest. "Historian." Still, wearing the police hat is a little like feeling the long green scarf wrapped around me. I peer out at Officer Salazar from under the brim.

I say, "Dawn Spurlock wasn't lying, when she called the police to the house. Daddy *was* rough with D.B. that night." I pause and swallow. "Dawn did the right thing. It was me who lied."

Officer Salazar looks serious. She picks her pencil up again, taps it on her desk, sighs. "It's a consequential thing to lie to the police."

"I know. D.B. didn't do anything wrong. He's a good person. He was trying hard at school. Now he's got sent back to that awful reform school. I deserve to be punished," I say.

She studies me. "Lying to the police, that could be a class D felony in Tennessee. People go to prison for it. Why did you say what you did?"

She sits patiently, waiting for me to collect myself. Finally, I say, "I was trying to protect my dad."

Officer Salazar nods. "You might ask yourself if being loyal to your papa is the best thing for everybody, including him. Maybe it is, maybe it isn't. But it doesn't excuse the lie."

I sit in silence.

Officer Salazar puts both elbows on her desk. "Miss Hawkins, it's no secret your papa is troubled. So far, he has done no serious harm, beyond running off with you overnight, or getting himself into one or two bar fights. And spending some time down here in jail with us. But roughing up your young friend, that's crossing a line. He's a boy. And from what I understand, he's a boy who has troubles of his own."

I put my face in my hands. "I know," I say. "Daddy's in the V.A. hospital now." My chin starts to tremble.

"Lyndie, I'll tell you something. We have Vietnam vets all over Love's Forge suffering like your papa. A whole generation of men saw things and did things during the war they can't let go of, you know? My own brother went over, and believe me, he was not the same when he got back. Have you talked to your grandparents about this? Your mama? You should. Have an honest talk. Everybody is on your side."

My head feels light. "I don't want to lose my dad," I say.

She stands up and comes around her desk. "I know you don't, honey." She takes her police cap off my head and pats my braid. "It was good you came down here. That took courage. But you shouldn't be talking to the police without a grown-up here."

"Am I going to be charged with a crime?"

"We'll sort that out later. Come on, it's dark. I'll drive you home."

Me and Dawn slide into Officer Salazar's cruiser and pull out of the station. The police radio crackles with officers trading dumb jokes.

Did you hear that the Energizer Bunny was arrested?

He was charged with battery.

Why did the cop sit on the toilet?

To do his—

"Hey, knock it off. I've got kids in here!" Officer Salazar yells into her speaker.

I lean close to Dawn. "I couldn't have forced my legs to walk through that door without you, Dawn," I say. "I guess like Lady says, you are a good influence on me. I should try to be more like you."

Dawn puts her knitting away and blinks at me. "I always thought that about *you*," she says.

"What?"

"Yeah. When I first saw you in third grade. You were always reading. Remember when I sat next to you at recess that first time? You were halfway through a whole library book about one single battle! You were so, like, passionate."

"The Battle of Shiloh." I remember.

"I wanted to be in your category," Dawn says. "The category of people who ask questions. You were always poking around underneath the surface to find out what was true. You didn't just swallow everything you were told. I loved that."

I pull my head out of my knitted scarf and meet her eyes.

"But I couldn't *really* be like you," she goes on. "I figured that out. All those questions about everything, they make me feel anxious. I like things, you know, more certain. That's why I started going to Math Maniacs. In math, you know what's right or wrong."

Dawn puts her two wooly arms around me and gives me a strong hug. "I even started doing Hungry Honeys because of you," she says. "I wanted to be *completely* involved in something." She holds on tight, wrapping me in her lopsided Christmas sweater. Her hair smells like buttery cookies, the sweater smells like rose soap.

I'd forgotten how good it felt to be hugged by Dawn.

When I climb out of the cruiser, I'm still hurting and sad. But this kind has a different feel from the bottled-up, unspoken kind. It's a sad you can breathe through.

CHAPTER TWENTY-FIVE

After Officer Salazar drops me off, I go right upstairs and open a blank spiral notebook laid out on my claw-foot desk. I have some letters to write.

First: to D.B.'s foster mom. I tell her about how D.B. was getting tutored by Dawn night and day to bring himself up two whole grade levels, to Algebra 1. How he was memorizing vocabulary to make A's in English and pass his end-of-seventh-grade test. "D.B. was persistent about signing people up for kickboxing," I write. "He was truly sorry he set your house on fire. Sometimes, when you're sad, or angry, or confused, you can act out and make bad choices."

My hands hover over my notebook. What I have to say to her next, I'm not sure how to write. I know, no matter how Lady feels about sharing personal family details with strangers—I have to write to Mrs. Bigwitch about Daddy. I feel that she will understand.

I write and write, crossing out whole sentences, balling up my paper, and starting again, until the words sound honest. When I've read my letter three times to make sure I put down what's closest to the truth, I go to my bedside drawer and find the paper Dawn gave me with Mrs. Bigwitch's address.

I tuck the letter into an envelope and lick the glue.

One more to go. I take up my pen again.

Dear PeeWee,

I stop and chew on the end of my braid. Will PeeWee think I'm stupid for what I'm about to say? Will he make fun of me?

I wanted to tell you, first, I'm so sorry
your dad died in the war. And second, even
though my dad looks okay on the outside, and
we're lucky to have him alive, that he's never
been 100 percent happy and easy long as I've
known him. PeeWee, I've learned that this

war my dad fought in, and so did yours, has
touched about every person in Love's Forge,
and probably far beyond that too. I have an
idea, that we kids of veterans should be loyal
to each other. We should not allow this war,
that was over ten years ago and that both our
dads sacrificed for, to go on and on between
us. We are on the same side. I hope you see it
that way too.

> *Your friend (I hope),*
> *Lyndie Hawkins*

The letter to PeeWee, I fold up and seal with a piece of Scotch tape to take it to school tomorrow. Mrs. Bigwitch's letter, I decide to mail right now. I rummage back in my bedside drawer looking for a stamp book. Then I go down our gravel drive and put her letter in the mailbox next to the gate.

"We have an appointment with Pastor Jinks today, after school," Lady says in the kitchen Friday morning. We're all scarfing down Pop-Tarts and Shredded Wheat at the kitchen table, which is an all-time first. Our "family break-fasts" have gotten simplified lately.

"What? Again? What did I do?"

Lady's hands are nervous, buttering her toast, her movements sharp. "We'll all be attending, this time. Me and your ma and Grandpa Tad. Two thirty." She has two swipes of bright pink in her cheeks, and she won't meet my eye.

"But why?"

A flicker of what looks like remorse passes through her eyes before she turns away. She's halfway out the door, calling up the stairs to Ma. "Hurry up, Rainbow, you're slow as molasses!"

A whole caboodle of terrible upends over my head. All three of them and Pastor Jinks?

The screen door bangs and Lady's Cadillac starts up.

I've been getting in trouble at school ever since I first set foot on Covenant property. For fighting with PeeWee. For daydreaming through boring classes. For not "fitting in" with the nice girls. Covenant also has a strict policy against lying, and by now, everybody and their pet cow knows I lied to the police.

The only reason Pastor Jinks would call us all down there is this: I am finally getting kicked out of Covenant for good.

So it doesn't matter if I do or don't make things right

with PeeWee—if I'm going to get expelled, our war is officially over. All that's left is the principle of it.

I guess the principle turns out to be important enough on its own. I catch up with PeeWee as he's about to round the corner into Advanced English. "Wait up, PeeWee." I pinch hold the tail of his blazer, and he spins round, eyes widening when he sees me.

"I may as well tell you now, since I don't know if I'll be here tomorrow. I'm sorry I punched your nose." I shove my letter at him. "That was wrong."

PeeWee looks stumped. We're not exactly in the habit of civil words. But he takes the letter.

"Even though you put gum in my hair, I ought not to have hit you," I say.

PeeWee stands there goggling at me.

"Of course," I add. "If you want to say you are sorry about the gum in my braid, I would totally accept your apology. It took two hours and a full jar of peanut butter to get all that Wrigley's Spearmint out."

Now PeeWee looks baffled. "A jar full of peanut butter?" he says.

"Yeah. It's the only way to get gum out of hair. You have to really glob it on and then comb it through."

PeeWee thinks. "That makes sense."

"It does?"

"Yeah. Gum is hydrophobic, it doesn't dissolve in water; that's why you can chew it. So when you put the oily peanut butter on it, which is also hydrophobic, they stick to each other. And the peanut butter makes the gum stiff. I bet mayonnaise would work too."

I'm flabbergasted. "How the heck do you know this?"

"It's chemistry. Simple."

That I have completely misjudged PeeWee hits me. No wonder he's in Advanced English. I never paid attention to him as anything but someone to fight with. It dawns on me that he may actually be a brain. Only he doesn't ever show it.

Honestly, I think my feelings about PeeWee started to change after I saw that picture of him in his hospital crib with all the tubes. It's hard to feel mean about someone who was once a three-pound baby with a wire stuck up his tiny little nose, fighting to survive. "But the letter," I say. "Actually, it's about something more important than gum and peanut butter."

PeeWee doesn't look like he's going to apologize. So I turn and walk away fast. I don't want him to see how embarrassed I am.

I swear, I think I hear him mumble "Okay, I'm sorry too" behind me. But I can't be sure.

When I get to the front office for our meeting with Pastor Jinks after school, Lady and Ma and Grandpa Tad are not there yet. Miss Smitty radiates disapproval; she aims her skinny finger at one of the chairs outside the pastor's door. "Sit," she mouths at me. Somebody else is already occupying the other chair.

The *somebody else* is a phenomenon. This man has an eagle's beak nose and a tattooed scrawl under one eye. When I perch on the seat next to him, that tattooed eye gives me a full up and down, from my polished loafers to my pressed school blazer, then fastens on my face.

I can't help gaping up at him. His shirt cuffs are rolled, and he's got another tattoo on his wrist, geometric shapes that go together to form a regal bird, its beak wide open and its wings fiercely spread. I swear I never saw muscles like the ones he's got; it's like there could be three separate forearms twined together and bulging under his skin. And I for sure never saw a person like him anywhere inside the walls of Covenant Methodist Academy. He twitches an eyebrow at me.

Oh.

I recognize that eyebrow. It's genetic.

All those hours and hours of microfilm I pored over in

the library, all the stories about *bolo punches* and *liver shots*, it's like I conjured this person right into the front office at Covenant Academy by some kind of research magic.

I only realize I'm gaping when he says in a gravelly voice that is not exactly friendly, "My sis used to tell me when my jaw was hanging open like that, *a fine way to trap gnats.*" Which makes me snap my mouth shut. But what does Screaming Eagle have to do here today with me getting kicked out of Covenant?

Before I can ask, Lady and Ma and Grandpa Tad arrive. As I'm standing up, Officer Salazar comes in behind them, handcuffs jangling. Am I getting arrested for lying to the police? Pastor Jinks opens his office door and waves us in.

It's a tight squeeze to get the six of us stuffed into the pastor's small office. And then once we're all crammed into our chairs, everybody has to get his or her cup of coffee, with their exact personal ratio of cream and sugar, balanced precariously on a china saucer, before anyone can get to the point.

"I asked you here today because as we all know, recent events have taken a very worrisome turn," Pastor Jinks says. My chair is between Screaming Eagle and Ma. Ma takes my hand and squeezes.

Here it comes.

"We're here to discuss the problem of Dee-Ell, of course."

Lady looks mystified. "Dee-Ell?"

"D.B.," says the pastor.

"Oh," Lady says. "Mr. Bloodboil."

The pastor pauses. Maybe thinking he didn't hear Lady right. "Mr. Baily," he says. "Yes. D.B. We're very concerned about what happened." Lady flushes deep pink when he says this. She pulls a fan from her purse and starts waving it at her face.

Ma laces her fingers between mine. Grandpa Tad shoots me a sympathetic look.

I bet Screaming Eagle is here today to press charges against me—for endangering his nephew by lying to the police. *Class D felony,* Officer Salazar said. Will they ship me off to reform school too?

Grandpa Tad is saying something about working with Child Protective Services. He's talking about a *guardian ad litem,* whatever that is, and something or other a judge has agreed to. *Working with a lawyer who specializes in juvenile cases*—I catch that much. Ma is squeezing my hand so tight. Her eyes are brimming.

Officer Salazar says something about having a lot of experience with juvenile court and being willing to speak on behalf of something. Lady looks like she's about to burst into tears.

I picture D.B. putting his head down on his desk, motioning me down too. Saying about Pure Visions: *Kids die there*.

Lady has been fussing and fanning and blinking. Her shoulders are no longer ramrod straight. I notice she doesn't even have her sweater buttoned up the front straight.

"A minute," she says. She's breathless. "I feel I need to say something." All eyes turn to her.

"I want to apologize to Officer Salazar," she says in a wavery voice. "I was so distraught about my son, the night you were called, I don't believe I was thinking clearly. Tyrus was out of control. He is not well. I want to say it here, for all of us. Daxx is a good boy. He deserves a chance to make something of himself." She fans herself rapidly. Exhales. It seems like she's finished, but then she goes on. "I want to apologize to my granddaughter as well." Lady turns to me. Her eyes spill over. She drops the fan to fumble in her bag for a handkerchief. "I should never have allowed or encouraged you to betray your friend," she chokes out, blotting at her eyes. "You are better than that. I know it. We all know it."

The pastor sets his cup down and clears his throat. Everybody shifts in their chairs. Nobody speaks for a long minute. "Thank you, Mrs. Hawkins," the pastor says at last. "We appreciate that. One of our current objectives, as we discussed by phone, is to get D.B. released from Pure Visions into temporary custody of his uncle, Mr. Driver, here."

Wait, what?

"Tad and I have discussed it, and we will pay all legal fees incurred to secure Daxx's permanent release," Lady says. She blows her nose, delicately.

Screaming Eagle nods and unlatches his briefcase. He pulls some papers out and hands them to Grandpa Tad. "I got us a two-bedroom apartment," he says. "Near the center of town."

"That's excellent news," says Pastor Jinks. "D.B. can finish the year out here at Covenant. We'll get him right back in school and caught up with as little delay as possible."

"For the longer term," Grandpa Tad says, "we may be able to arrange a kind of joint custody with Janet Bigwitch. We've been consulting with D.B.'s social worker."

"Um," I say. "I don't follow what is happening."

All the grown-ups turn to look at me.

Grandpa Tad says, "Sugar, *you* asked me to look into this, getting D.B. out of Pure Visions. And your grandma explained—"

Lady looks flustered. "Ah. Tad. Lyndie and I had hardly a moment to exchange two words."

True. Lady and I haven't convened for our after-supper "tea and cookies in the parlor" all week. My heart contracts one notch. Is it possible I've missed our nightly tea and cookies?

"The short version is," Ma says gently, "D.B. will be released from Pure Visions into the temporary custody of his uncle." She smiles at Screaming Eagle. "Who has generously offered to move to Love's Forge for now, so that D.B. can finish out his school year. After that, D.B. may be able to go live with Mrs. Bigwitch. Or Mr. Driver and Mrs. Bigwitch might share custody. Or maybe D.B.'s mother can even be located. We'll see."

"I've got plans to open a boxing studio here," Screaming Eagle says.

"Grandpa Tad," I say. "You did it? You got him out?"

"You started the ball rolling, Lyndie. I applied a little force to move the ball along so it didn't quit."

Kinetic energy. The ball will roll D.B. right out of Pure Visions, and along the curly curving roads to Love's Forge. I'm so relieved, I feel the floor rocking under my feet.

D.B. is free.

But what about me?

"Grandpa Tad, are you going to argue my case in court? Will I have to plead guilty to a Class D felony?"

"What felony, sugar?"

"For lying to the police."

Grandpa Tad looks perplexed.

"How about we arrange for you to do some community service," Officer Salazar says. "The homeless veterans' council downtown is looking for volunteers."

"I advise you to take that deal," Grandpa Tad says. "Because frankly, I'm not sure you can afford me."

CHAPTER TWENTY-SIX

Daddy completes six weeks of sessions of his three-times-a-week out-patient treatment. Ma goes with him every Tuesday. And even I went twice. Lady has not one word of objection about us going to counseling. Daddy talks about his grief over Trilby dying. He talks about using liquor to dull down and camouflage all kinds of pain. He talks about his confusion over the Vietnam War, and his anxiety that kept him pacing, and having too much time on his hands to think about bad stuff when he was out of work. How sometimes he blacked out and couldn't remember what he had done.

He still has good days and less good days. But he's better. One Sunday, we take another road trip.

This time, Lady does not object up one side and down the other.

This time, we take the Cadillac instead of the Blue Bullet, to fit us all. Me, Daddy, Ma, and D.B.

Lady's fussing is mild as milk when she hands me my suitcase and Daddy throws his backpack and Ma's overnight bag into the trunk.

This trip is in honor of Veterans Day, which happens the next day, on Monday, November 11. First, we plan to drive to Cherokee, North Carolina, to see Janet Bigwitch. And then after that, to the East Tennessee State Veterans Cemetery outside Knoxville to participate in a memorial for the veterans who fought in all the wars.

As we pull out of the drive, we spot Grandpa Tad out in front of the barn with Hoopdee. He's got wood planks set up on two sawhorses. He's building me a tree house to go in the apple tree by the back porch. "Tell Lady we'll be back in time for supper, Monday," Ma calls out the car window to Grandpa.

I'm positive we will be.

Up on the high ridge road we pass through the deep shade of the forest, sunlight dappling the road.

D.B. is with me in the backseat. "Tell me again what she said," he wheedles, passing me a purple jujube.

I must've told the story of Grandpa Tad's many long conversations with D.B.'s foster mother, Janet, embellishing to keep myself from dying of multiple repetition syndrome, until I'm not completely certain what's fact and what's fiction anymore.

"Janet said she always wanted a foster son with an exceedingly magnificent and varied vocabulary, resulting in many A-pluses."

"And a *sur-plus* of jewelry," Daddy puts in over his shoulder.

"She said she's thought about you every single minute since the last time she saw you in court."

"And was determined," Daddy says, "that someday, someway, she'd have the opportunity to get you a decent haircut."

"She said there is nothing to forgive you for, and she hopes you'll forgive *her*."

"She said that?"

"Grandpa Tad told her not to worry, as you are incapable of holding any grudge longer than two weeks plus one day. Which I told Grandpa was my observation from *very personal experience*."

"You were being loyal, Lyndie," D.B. says. "I get that. Let bygones be bygones. Leave the past where it belongs."

"That's a philosophy to live by," Daddy says.

"Mr. Handy says, those that forget the past will be stuck perpetually making the same mistakes over and over," I argue.

"If he really does say that, he is massacring the original," Ma says.

"*Massacre*." D.B. hands me another jujube. "*To inflict a heavy defeat upon.* Hey, could we focus on me, please? What else did Janet say?"

D.B. has not talked to Janet directly except for only once on the phone since he came back to live in Love's Forge with Screaming Eagle. I chew, thinking. "Well, Janet said when all the legal paperwork stuff is done, you can stay with Uncle Screaming Eagle every school year so you can graduate from Covenant, and summers with her in Cherokee. She told Grandpa Tad she loves you and misses you."

"She said that?"

"I'm sure that part is one hundred percent factual."

Out the window, the last bursts of red and orange fall colors fly by like swaths of flame. The trees will be dropping their leaves soon. We round a corner, and in my mind I see a young doe raise her head out of the brush, snout quivering and brown eyes alert, exactly like Velvet. The sun breaks through the clouds as we drive by.

"I can't believe your grandpa is maybe getting Pure Visions closed down for good," D.B. says.

"It's Ma working on it too! Tell him, Ma." I tap her shoulder.

Ma twists around to face us. "I'm helping Lyndie's

grandpa get all the paperwork organized. We're partnering with the ACLU. Pure Visions ought to have been shut down a long time ago. I swear I'll see it done."

Ma has found her passion again for activism. When she's not working directly on D.B.'s case, or going to counseling with Daddy, or selling foundation garments at Miller's Department Store, she's volunteering to make phone calls about all kinds of civil rights abuses to raise money for the ACLU. She hasn't had a headache in a month.

"There's a whole bunch of boys who are going to thank you guys for that," D.B. says.

When we pull into the long driveway at Janet Bigwitch's wood-frame house in Cherokee, it's a cozy two-story nestled in a thicket of trees with a stream running behind. The wood shingle on the top story looks new. "That front flower border could use some tender loving care," I say. "How green is your thumb, D.B.?"

"A little less green than your envy of my straight A's this year," D.B. says.

I climb out of the car, and so does Ma, but Daddy and D.B. sit there, staring at the house.

I lean my elbows on the open window and look into D.B.'s face. "There's something to be said for straight B's," I tell him. "You still have stars to reach for."

"Yes," D.B. says vaguely. "How will I ever escape the prison of my own perfection?"

His features are twisted into a complicated expression of mixed-up hope and sorrow and apprehension. "Wow," he breathes. "I miss Trilby so bad."

After a minute, Daddy says, "I miss him too, son."

"I never let myself say that before. Look at that busted stair up to the porch. Trilby would have fixed that right away."

"He did have a talent for carpentry," Daddy says.

"He taught me how to do a crescent kick. And some of the Cherokee alphabet."

"He taught me grace under pressure." Daddy unbuckles his seat belt. "I'm still working on that one."

"Dawn can knit you a special scarf for that, Daddy," I say. "Mine sure helps me."

The front door opens and a lady I remember from the funeral comes out onto the porch. Daddy jumps out of the Cadillac and strides toward her, climbs past the busted step and takes both the hands she holds out to him. She looks up at him, and I can see even from here, she is struggling to stay composed. "I'm glad to see you, Tyrus," she says. "Alive and well."

"Better every day," Daddy says.

And then she's running to the car and opening the side door and pulling D.B. up and into her arms. They stand there on the gravel drive, and there's a bit of snuffling and murmuring. D.B. is taller than his foster mother by a foot, and certainly fatter.

But somehow they seem to fit just right in each other's arms.

In time for our Monday dinner, we pull into the driveway past our new American flag. Replacing that beat-up old flag was the first thing Daddy did when he started to feel better. The colors are as bright and true as I guess the very first flown American flag was, sewn from a captain's coat and soldiers' shirts and the wives' petticoats. I love that story so much. How all the scraps from the many different people went into making something beautiful. A true and beautiful thing that seems like, if we're careful with it, it could last forever.

ACKNOWLEDGMENTS

This book would never have made it from mind to page without the generosity of many other children's book authors. Donna Gephart and Linda Marlow took me under their wings when I was the hapless but hopeful new kid at writer school, and have never stopped cheerleading my efforts. Marjetta Geerling's early enthusiasm made me believe I might actually amount to something someday. Joyce Sweeney, Jamie Morris, and Lorin Oberweger all read versions and stretched my understanding of craft and what a novel could be. Jill Nadler gave me the pep talk I desperately needed at exactly the right moment. Stacie Ramey's dedication, talent, and passion have been constant bright stars to light the way.

My SCBWI Florida Wellington and Palm Beach Gardens

critique groups have been an ongoing source of camaraderie and good sense: Bless you all. Debra Getts and Liza Parfomak pulled out all the stops when I was down to the wire and spent precious winter holidays reading and emailing sensitive, smart, and invaluable critiques. My online MG writers group at InkedVoices patiently read and reread chapters until they were finally banged into shape—thank you Mindy Alyse Weiss and Susan Verini. Bethany Hegedus's Writing Barn in Austin, Texas, was a place of magic, inspiration, and fellowship. And the Florida SCBWI is an amazing organization, thanks to the tireless efforts of so many writers and illustrators; I am boundlessly grateful to all of you, but special thanks to Linda Rodriguez Bernfeld and Dorian Cirrone for all you do for your Florida family.

Camilla Griggers and Marni Borek dropped everything and drove me up Highway 1 from L.A. to Big Sur for my first ever writers' conference—a road trip that launched me into a new calling. Rick and Stephanie Shepherd, Sandra Tepper, and Steve Ellman: my thanks for many years of love, friendship, and lively discussions on topics literary and otherwise. You are all an inspiration.

To Kristin Halbrook Vincent, my first literary agent: endless gratitude for your editorial guidance, sense of humor, and imagination. Bob Diforio, my current agent, much appreciation for your good cheer and confidence.

Bottomless thanks are due to my patient and persistent editor, Kathy Dawson, for her belief that the kernel of this book could be tended into something deeper and richer. Kathy has taught me a great deal about how to shape a story. I couldn't have dreamed up a better editor; I am beyond grateful for her tireless attention to detail and her passion for what matters in fictional worlds. Thanks too, to copyeditor Regina Castillo for her sensitive and exacting pass through many versions of this manuscript, to book designer Jenny Kelly, to jacket designer Dana Li, to my publicist Kaitlin Kneafsey, and to the rest of the team at Penguin, who do so much to get the right books into the hands of young readers.

I had countless conversations about fiction writing, screenwriting, and publishing with my brilliant sister, Susan Shepherd, unflagging in her faith in me—Sue, your encouragement has meant everything.

Amy D'Arecca, soul mate, I've lost track of the number of long writing weekends you've organized (and paid for!) in hotels around the country—man, we've had fun. You've been my number one fan, and you know that I am yours, always.

DISCUSSION QUESTIONS

I. On page 260, Lyndie muses, "I think the truth is a place you can only move toward, like walking toward the horizon. Even though you know you'll never get all the way there." How does this insight speak to Lyndie's journey, her coming of age? What has she learned about the truth, justice, and not giving up in the face of difficulty?

2. Are there any people in history or living today who have helped shape your own understanding of what is true or false in our world? Who, how, and why? In what sense do we never "get all the way there" in our understanding of history and ourselves?

3. How has the Vietnam War affected Lyndie's mother and father, and how has it affected her?

4. What does Lyndie mean on page 268 when she questions, "How can I explain my family? Or how I've been caught in the middle of it so long, I can't clearly see the links in the history chain?"

5. What role does the location of Love's Forge and its role in history (the Civil War, the Trail of Tears) play in this story? What role does it play in Lyndie's family's history?

6. How does Lyndie's understanding of Southern history conflict with Lady's understanding?

7. In what ways are Lyndie's friends Dawn and D.B. alike and not, and how do they push Lyndie to view her world differently?

8. What other characters challenge Lyndie, and how does her opinion of them change over time?

9. What different types of loyalty does Lyndie learn about over the course of the novel? Do you think she has a clear-cut definition of loyalty by the end? Why or why not?

FOR A COMPREHENSIVE TEACHING AND DISCUSSION GUIDE, VISIT
http://gailshepherdauthor.com/teachers/.